ORPHAN ELEVEN

GENNIFER CHOLDENKO

WENDY
LAMB
BOOKS

Text copyright © 2020 by Gennifer Choldenko
Jacket art copyright © 2020 by Iacopo Bruno

All rights reserved. Published in the United States by Wendy Lamb Books, an imprint of Random House Children's Books, a division of Penguin Random House LLC, New York.

Wendy Lamb Books and the colophon are trademarks of Penguin Random House LLC.

Visit us on the Web! rhcbooks.com

Educators and librarians, for a variety of teaching tools, visit us at RHTeachersLibrarians.com

Library of Congress Cataloging-in-Publication Data
Names: Choldenko, Gennifer, author.
Title: Orphan eleven / Gennifer Choldenko.
Description: First edition. | New York : Wendy Lamb Books, [2020] |
Includes bibliographical references. | Summary: In 1939, after cruel treatment at her orphanage renders her mute, Lucy runs away and joins the circus, working with the elephants and unaware that the orphanage matrons are hunting for her.
Identifiers: LCCN 2019023493 (print) | LCCN 2019023494 (ebook) |
ISBN 978-0-385-74255-9 (hardcover) | ISBN 978-0-375-99064-9 (library binding) |
ISBN 978-0-385-74256-6 (paperback) | ISBN 978-0-307-97578-2 (ebook)
Subjects: CYAC: Orphans—Fiction. | Orphanages—Fiction. | Selective mutism—Fiction. | Runaways—Fiction. | Circus—Fiction. | Elephants—Fiction. | Human experimentation in medicine—Fiction.
Classification: LCC PZ7.C446265 Or 2020 (print) |
LCC PZ7.C446265 (ebook) | DDC [Fic]—dc23

Printed in the United States of America
10 9 8 7 6 5 4 3 2 1
First Edition

To Meredith Bullock, my "big sister,"
to David Macaulay, who believed in me,
and to Alan Blum. He knows why.

CONTENTS

. . . .

PART THREE

PART ONE

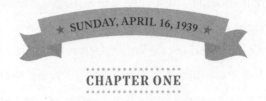

CHAPTER ONE

HOME FOR FRIENDLESS CHILDREN

Most kids who ran away got caught. Or they came back on their own sorry feet. Nobody had anywhere to run to or they wouldn't be in the Home for Friendless Children in the first place.

But it wasn't every day they were allowed outside the gate.

Even so, Lucy wasn't about to run. After five years of looking at that wrought-iron fence, it had become as much a part of her as the metal cot she slept on. There wasn't anything else that was hers. Unless you counted a folded piece of paper, the list of this week's vocabulary words, the blue button, and the baby tooth in her pocket, and the extra pencil stub stuck in the hem of her dress.

What with the downpour, today was a lousy day to run anyway. Rain dripped off Lucy's chin and flattened the thick

3

mass of her curly red hair. Rain made her stockings squishy in her too-small shoes. Rain soaked her wool coat, making it feel like the weight of her eleven years was on her back.

It wasn't like she'd get far with Matron Mackinac not more than five feet from her. Mackinac had piercing eyes, lips the color of dead fish, and a heart like a lump of coal—black and dusty and small.

Lucy had trusted Mackinac once. She'd tried her best to please her by coming early to choir, earning first desk in the schoolroom, and scrubbing the muddy footprints from the hall outside her office. She'd even told the other orphans not to bad-mouth Mrs. Mackinac. Now she hated herself for it.

For the last year and a half, Mackinac had humiliated Lucy every time she opened her mouth. "What a disappointment you are, and I had such high hopes," Mackinac had said in front of everyone. "You'll never amount to anything." The harder Lucy tried, the more Mackinac mocked her.

Where Mackinac had only occasionally noticed her before, now she singled her out for daily torment. In the dark orphanage nights, Lucy wondered if Mackinac and Miss Holland, the lady from the university, were right when they said something was terribly wrong with Lucy. *"You are an embarrassment to the orphanage. Everyone can see it."*

Now Mackinac hovered over Lucy and Bald Doris as they shoveled river sand into burlap bags to staunch leaks in the staff house.

But they were outside the fence and the clean smell of the

rain and the glimpse of the world beyond the trees sent a wild thrill through Lucy.

If Lucy's best friend, Emma, had been there, they could have run together. Emma saved Lucy a place in line, shared the handfuls of sugar she got from the cook, and made Lucy laugh when she missed her big sister, Dilly. "Everybody misses someone. Best not to dwell," Emma said.

But last week a lady had signed the papers to adopt Emma. With Emma gone, every day was orphanage gray.

Lucy did not want to go anywhere with Bald Doris. Doris was a girl you made sure was in front of you in line so that you could see what she was up to. She lied as easily as other girls tied their shoes. About as often, too.

The rain hammered down on Lucy's head and battered her shoulders.

In weather like this, it didn't matter if Lucy spoke or not. No one could hear what anyone said.

Matron Mackinac pulled her oxfords out of the mud and slipped a cough drop between the gap in her teeth. "Lucy, get working!"

Lucy was shoveling. Bald Doris was leaning against the wall. But as usual, it was Lucy whom Mackinac scolded.

"We aren't even halfway—" Rain drowned out Mackinac's words. "Stay here," she shouted, and ran across the grass to the boys' house.

Lucy's heart knocked like a woodpecker in her chest. Orphans were never left alone outside the fence.

If only Lucy had had time to plan. Then she'd know which direction to run. No matter which way she chose, Bald Doris would tell Mackinac, but Lucy had fast feet.

Only now it was too late. Mackinac was coming out of the boys' cottage. Lucy had lost her chance.

The disappointment tasted like blood in Lucy's mouth.

Mackinac struggled to close the rain-swollen door. Next to her were two boys carrying shovels. One boy was Lucy's size—small for an eleven-year-old. He had dark hair and a bounce to his walk like the ground sprang him up with every step. The other was as big as a barn door, with falling-down trousers that seemed to need his regular attention. Both had on the charcoal-gray coats all the orphans wore.

The bigger boy nodded to Doris. Doris made a face at him. The boys dug in, shovelheads clinking against each other in the river sand.

Matron Mackinac walked along the line of sandbags set against the side of the house, one hand on the skirt of her umbrella to keep the wind from turning it inside out. She slid the candy around in her mouth, her eyes flicking between the girls and the boys. "Don't move. I'll be right back," she said, and hurried off, her oxfords making squelching noises as she pulled her feet out of the mud.

Lucy took a step forward. But the wind rose, shoving her back, and her right foot returned to its place by her left.

Then the wind died down and the sound of the river filled her ears. All of the awful things that had happened to Lucy at the orphanage came rushing through her head: the humiliating lessons with Miss Holland, the cruelty of Matron Mackinac, the cold sweats on the mornings Mackinac read the list of orphans to be sent to reform school.

Lucy took off across the wet grass and through the trees. She leapt the ditch to the dirt road, her legs sailing under her.

She had just gotten to the river when she heard pounding feet behind her.

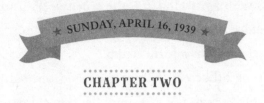

CHAPTER TWO

"SMARTEST MAN IN CHICAGO"

Lucy stole a look over her shoulder to see how close Mackinac was.

But it was the big boy, with one hand gripping his trousers, followed by Bald Doris. The smaller boy was gaining on Lucy, his arms pumping with effort.

Mackinac had sent them to catch her. Lucy forced her feet to run faster.

The smaller boy pounded at her heels. "Wait! Hey!"

Get away! The words floated through Lucy's head, then slipped back down her throat.

"We're coming with you!" he shouted.

Lucy stopped, her throat burning. She bent over to catch her breath and got a good look at the bigger boy. His ears stuck out of hair that needed cutting, but his blue eyes were unafraid, as if running away were a natural thing to do, like a burp.

Bald Doris was right behind him, scratching her head. The matron had shaved her hair to get rid of lice, but the ointment they rubbed on her scalp made her itch.

The smaller boy had city in him. He was more like the kids Lucy knew back home in Chicago. He squinted at Lucy. "Where we going?"

Cold, wet, and hungry, with blisters forming on her feet, the only idea Lucy could come up with was to find her sister, Dilly, who would be seventeen and nearly a grown-up now.

But Dilly was in Chicago. Lucy had no idea where in the city she lived . . . or even if she was still there.

The smaller boy's bright eyes grew large, scrutinizing Lucy. "Let's introduce ourselves. I'm Nico. That's Eugene." He pointed to the bigger boy.

Doris stepped forward. "I'm Doris. Don't call me Bald Doris."

"Eugene's sister?" Nico asked.

"Half sister," Bald Doris corrected him.

Lucy inspected Eugene. He was twice the size of Doris, but they both had the same round face and fuzzy yellow hair on their arms.

Nico, the dark-haired boy, nodded. "How do you do, Not-Bald-Doris."

Doris scowled.

Nico turned to Lucy, waiting for her to introduce herself.

Doris took a step forward. "Her name is Lucy," she said.

Nico nodded, his eyes asking the question Lucy didn't want to answer. Why hadn't Lucy said anything?

"Don't bother talking to her, because she won't say anything," Doris said.

Nico shrugged and they started walking again. The dark sky made the late afternoon seem like evening as they moved in and out of the trees on the side of the road. The lights of the cars shone long and low in the mist.

Nico hopped over a stone wall. Lucy and Eugene scrambled after him. Bald Doris was caught in the headlights as she tried to get a toehold.

The car didn't stop.

"We got to get moving," Nico said. "They'll send somebody after us."

"Matron Grundy," Eugene said with such certainty that Lucy wondered if he'd run away before.

Lucy and Nico walked together. Eugene stuck close to Doris.

"We'll find Frank and Alice," Nico announced.

Lucy glanced over at him. He seemed full to the brim with himself. Even so, she liked how confidently he said "Frank and Alice," as if he were reading the time from a clock.

"They your parents?" Doris asked.

"No," Nico said.

"Uncle and aunt?"

"Not exactly. Frank is the smartest man in Chicago."

Chicago. Frank and Alice lived in Chicago!

Lucy had been six when she'd left Chicago. She'd come to Riverport with her mama to join Mama's brand-new husband, Thomas Slater, but her big sister, Dilly, had not been with them. At the last minute there'd been no money for Dilly's ticket, so Dilly had stayed in Chicago with the neighbors, the Sokoloffs, to wait for Mama to wire money. Mama and Lucy had taken the train to meet Thomas Slater. But when they arrived, they found out everything he'd said was a lie. Mr. Slater had no home, no job, no car, and no money. But Mama loved him, so they stayed in Riverport and she got a job as quickly as she could. She found work as a maid for a lady who was very sick with tuberculosis, and then Mama got sick, too. Mama was terrified Lucy would catch TB, so Thomas Slater dropped her at the Home for Friendless Children. "Just until your mama gets back on her feet," he said.

At the orphanage, Lucy had sent two letters to Dilly at the Sokoloffs. The nice teacher, Miss Ellie, had given her the stamp and mailed the first one. But the envelope had come back stamped ADDRESSEE UNKNOWN, and Miss Ellie said there was no point in sending another.

After that Lucy made up a song for the postman and sang it to him as he walked along one side of the orphanage fence and she walked on the other. She sang that same song every day, until he'd agreed to take the second letter without a stamp or an envelope. That letter came back like the first: ADDRESSEE UNKNOWN. So Dilly wasn't living with the Sokoloffs, or the

Sokoloffs had moved. Either way, Lucy had no idea where Dilly was.

Now Doris asked, "How do we find Frank and Alice?"

"Hitch a ride to Chicago," Nico said.

Hope rose inside Lucy at the word "Chicago." Was Dilly still there?

The orphans moved onto the main highway, where there was a steady stream of cars. They were more likely to get caught out here, but how else could they get a ride?

The ditch that bordered the highway swelled with water. The air smelled new, and the sky was bigger than it had seemed in the stark orphanage yard.

Now that the wild chase was over, Lucy's toes stung in her too-tight shoes. Orphans' shoes were always too big or too small.

Nico ran in front, waving down the cars, but no one stopped.

Then Lucy took a turn. Three cars sped by, but the fourth, a pickup truck with loose hay flying out the back, was slowing.

Nico and Eugene grinned at Lucy as they ran toward the truck. But just as it pulled onto the shoulder, an old blue Ford rolled up behind it with Matrons Mackinac and Grundy inside.

"Run!" Nico shouted, taking off down the side bank. Lucy followed him, grabbing the roots of a bush to keep from slipping.

When she glanced back, she saw that Matron Mackinac

had hold of Bald Doris's ear. Bald Doris was pointing at them. She couldn't tattle fast enough.

"Lucy! Lucy!" the matrons shouted.

Lucy wondered why they didn't call anyone else's name.

The matrons began to run.

Mackinac pulled Doris along. Grundy was twice Mackinac's age, but she was remarkably fast.

"We'll double back." Nico grabbed Lucy's hand and pulled her around a clump of bushes and back up to the road, where the truck waited.

The pickup truck driver was standing outside. She was a girl barely older than they were, with a swollen stomach like a darning egg in her slender frame and large men's boots.

Lucy and Nico jumped into the back of the truck.

Eugene thundered down the road, sailing through the air toward Mackinac and Doris.

"No!" Mackinac shouted, ducking out of the way.

Eugene landed with a thud, missing both of them. But in her surprise, Mackinac lost her grip on Doris, and Eugene boosted her over his shoulder like a bundle of towels. He ran with her to the truck, heaved her in, and leapt up after her.

The pregnant girl slipped behind the wheel and the truck shot forward.

Lucy looked back at the matrons waving their hands in the air and shouting, "Stop!"

Eugene grinned at Nico. Bald Doris smiled as if this had been her idea.

Nico glared at Doris.

Doris frowned. "What was I supposed to do? She got ahold of my ear."

Nico rolled his eyes.

In the distance, Lucy saw Mackinac and Grundy jump into the Ford and gun it. But the Ford was old, and the pregnant girl drove fast. Soon the old blue car was no bigger than a thimble, and then it disappeared entirely.

The loose straw flew in their faces. Lucy's wet hair whipped around. In the scuffle, she had lost the tie that held it back. She stuck her hair inside her coat and settled against the cab between Eugene and Nico. Their legs were stretched out in front of them—all eight in a row. The cold air rushed by Lucy's wet clothes, making her shiver, but the warmth of the four of them sitting this way was something. It surely was.

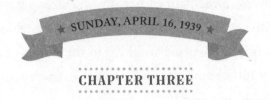
CHAPTER THREE

"NO ORPHAN BORROWS"

Lucy didn't think Matrons Mackinac and Grundy would waste more time looking for them. No one cared about orphans. That was why they were orphans. But it didn't seem to matter to the pregnant girl that they had lost sight of the blue Ford some time ago. She drove like a wheel girl for a bank robbery.

Lucy began watching for signs that might tell them where they were. FRESKET, DORIAN, CATWELL flew by. She didn't know any of those towns. They had studied geography, but only the state capitals, which now seemed foolish.

When enough of the straw in the back of the truck had blown away, Eugene found two folded burlap sacks, which he spread over them, tucking the edges under their legs.

The rain had stopped, but the clouds were dark and

threatening. Lucy wormed the paper out of her pocket and the pencil stub from the hem of her dress. The paper was damp, but not ruined. She smoothed it out, making a table with her legs. Her tiny handwriting wobbled in the swaying truck, and when they hit a bump, the tail of the *G* struck across the *C*. But you could still read it.

Chicago?

Eugene handed the paper to Nico. "We headed that way?"

"Yep," Nico said. His voice was sure, but his foot was fidgeting.

Thinking about Chicago had made Lucy feel powerful. But sitting in the truck with the wind in her face, she felt her insides shift like loose sand with nothing to bank against.

What was happening at the orphanage? Would they serve stew tonight? The stew was watery. But there were sweet carrots and sometimes a bite or two of gristle you could chew until bedtime.

The truck swayed and the farms sailed by, reminding Lucy of the train trip so long ago.

When she and Mama left Chicago, it had been winter, with snow-covered fields out the window. The train car was squeaky and cold. Mama had taken off Lucy's shoes and stuck her mittens on her toes. They had laughed at how silly her feet looked, ate butter sandwiches from Mama's basket, and played alphabet games, guessing the initials of the man Lucy would marry. It had felt strange not to have Dilly with them, like a stool with just two legs. Papa had died so long ago. It had been just the three of them, Lucy, Dilly, and Mama, for almost as long as Lucy could remember.

Still, Mama hadn't been worried. Her eyes glistened in a way that made her look more beautiful than tired. She'd splurged on lipstick, which she applied every few hours, rolling her lips together to spread the color. "We will all be together soon," she'd told Lucy, squeezing her hand.

Now Lucy glanced at Nico, then erased *Chicago,* the paper pressed against her knee, and wrote, *Frank and Alice?*

Nico smiled like he had just eaten a big meal and began rattling off facts. "Frank likes dollar pancakes piled this high." He gestured with his hand to his chin. "He takes two cubes of sugar in his coffee. He orders pie with a scoop of ice cream and gives me half. Alice is his best dame."

When Nico talked about Frank and Alice, his leg went still and his eyes took on a deeper color, more like the lake than the sky.

"Alice carries decks of cards in her purse. She pays me five cents to carry her hatboxes up the stairs. And she can spell any word backward."

Lucy settled back, listening. Soon, the motion of the truck and the stories about Frank and Alice lulled her to sleep.

When she woke, she smelled Mama's lipstick so intensely, she lurched forward, looking around for her.

Lucy used to dream of Mama and Dilly all the time. But

Mackinac had told her Mama had died. Lucy knew that was true because she'd seen for herself how sick Mama was. Besides, Mama would never have left her in the orphanage if she were alive. Mackinac said Lucy wouldn't see Dilly again, but Lucy didn't believe that. Mackinac's words had as much truth in them as supper stew had meat.

For the first few years at the orphanage, Lucy's insides had swelled every time the new-arrival bell rang, hoping for Dilly. Over time, the bell had lost its hold on her, until it was just another sound, like the tapping of the night matron's cane when she walked down the hall.

The truck rolled down a tree-lined street, then slowed to a stop. The cab door opened and the girl hopped out. "Hey, back there. I'm Bernadette."

Bernadette had long straight hair and a dress that was too big in the top and too tight across her belly. She smiled, revealing a mouth full of teeth that grew in all directions. "Got away pretty good."

"Yes, ma'am," Nico said.

"I was in that home for two years. Never took to Hannah Mackinac or Gertrude Grundy." Bernadette's eyes narrowed.

Bernadette was an orphan? Lucy and Nico exchanged a look.

"Recognized them coats," Bernadette said.

The coats had been purchased with a donation from the university. Woolen blankets, the new industrial-size stove, and

18

Matron Mackinac's caramels were also courtesy of the university. Whenever people from the university visited, the orphanage floors were scrubbed, windows cleaned, and doorknobs shined, and the orphans' choir sang them songs.

That was why it had been such a privilege to be picked for singing lessons by Miss Holland, the university lady. None of the other girls in choir had been singled out. Lucy had thought it was because she sang so well.

Soon she discovered that meeting with Miss Holland wasn't an honor, and it had nothing to do with singing. Lucy had never tried so hard to please anyone, repeating the words Miss Holland wanted her to say over and over again. But the harder she tried, the more Miss Holland shouted at her.

"Where you headed?" Bernadette asked.

"Chicago. To see Frank and Alice," Nico said.

Chicago. Lucy never tired of hearing this.

The girl whistled. "That's a ways. I can put you on the highway that leads there. Shouldn't take too long to get a ride. But you got to wait till morning. Too dangerous at night." She kneaded her lip with her teeth.

"That'll be fine, ma'am. Thank you," Nico said.

Bernadette nodded. "You can stay with me tonight, but you got to be quiet and do what I say." Her eyes narrowed. "No orphan borrows."

They all bobbed their heads.

At the orphanage, a Christmas orange, a scrap of ribbon,

a drawing, or a button always got pinched. Girls would pull down your underwear if they thought you had something hidden in there.

The orphanage was rife with bullies and broken promises. Lucy had learned to keep her head down and never let anyone see what was in her pockets. When Emma arrived, Lucy found a true friend. Emma was the only girl she could completely trust—the only one who Lucy showed her pocket treasures to.

But even Emma didn't understand why Mackinac had turned on Lucy so completely.

Bernadette's eyes grew small. "I've been known to track a person to the dark side of the earth they got something belongs to me, you understand?"

They all nodded.

"What are your names?" Bernadette asked.

"I'm Nico. That's Eugene. This here is Lucy." Nico pointed to each of them. Lucy was glad Nico did the talking; then her silence wasn't so noticeable.

"And that's Eugene's sister, Not-Bald-Doris," Nico continued.

"*Doris,* not Bald Doris." Doris glowered at Nico. "I won't be bald forever."

Bernadette nodded. "We got to be real careful. But"—she smiled her crooked-teeth smile—"I slipped folks in before. Just remember, orphans are easy to spot. Them coats. That lice cut."

Bald Doris's cheeks turned pink. She scratched at her hairless head.

Bernadette let down the truck bed and they got out. Then she went back to the cab, taking steps that meant business in her big men's boots. She returned with a bottle of milk.

Lucy and Nico stared. Eugene's mouth dropped open. Bald Doris reached out two trembling hands.

Bernadette raised an eyebrow. "Know how to share?"

Lucy, Nico, and Eugene nodded. Doris's eyes were riveted to the milk bottle, but she nodded, too.

Bernadette handed the bottle to Bald Doris. Doris held the cold milk in two hands, her throat working hard to handle the gushing stream of liquid.

"Hey." Nico elbowed her. Bald Doris tightened her grip and drank without stopping, until Eugene yanked the bottle away.

Bald Doris wiped her milky mouth with the back of her hand, moaning with pleasure.

They all looked at the milk. Three-quarters gone.

Bernadette's eyes went narrow as buttonholes. "That the way you follow directions?"

"Yes, ma'am." Doris smiled politely.

Nico snorted.

Eugene offered the bottle to Lucy without drinking any himself. Lucy's eyes widened, but she did not question his generosity. She took the bottle and drank the milk, which went down cool, thick, and buttery in her parched throat.

But after two good swigs she forced herself to stop and handed the bottle back to Eugene, who gave it to Nico.

Nico took his share and then returned the milk to Eugene, who drank the last few sips.

Bernadette stared at Nico, her jaw hard. "Bald Doris ain't going to my place. Got a baby coming and a husband who won't be home until December. I can't have a kid who don't listen."

Nico nodded, his left eye twitching.

"My hair's growing back." Bald Doris's voice wavered.

Bernadette shook her head. "Hair's fine. It's your heart I don't much care for."

Doris's chin jutted out. "I gave it back like you said!"

Bernadette and Lucy exchanged a look.

"What? I did." Bald Doris stamped her foot.

Bernadette's brow furrowed. "You took three times your share. Would have drunk the entire bottle if Eugene hadn't yanked it out of your hands."

"Well, I was going to give it back. *He* didn't give me a chance." Bald Doris pointed at Eugene.

Lucy glared at Doris.

"I've met plenty of girls like you. Would lie about the number of toes on their feet. Can't have you at my place," Bernadette said firmly.

Large tears began flowing down Bald Doris's cheeks, leaving pink lines on her dirty face. "It wasn't my fault," she sobbed.

"Where will she go?" Nico's voice squeaked.

The question hung in the air like a bad smell.

Bernadette surveyed them, ignoring Doris. "You take her with you, you won't make it," she said in her gravelly voice.

Lucy shuddered. As annoying as Doris was, they couldn't leave her.

Eugene stepped forward. "There's a good part inside her. She just don't like to show it much. I'll watch her, ma'am. You got my word."

"I sure hope you got some other family besides her," Bernadette said.

"I'll see to it she does what you ask." Eugene's voice was charged.

Lucy took a step toward Eugene. They stood shoulder to shoulder. Nico's eyes darted around, searching for a way out. Then he stepped forward, too.

"All of us, or none of us, miss," Nico said.

Bernadette's eyes shifted and then hardened. She turned her back on them and walked to the cab.

Lucy's stomach sank.

Please!

The word climbed up her throat.

Nico and Eugene looked at each other.

"She's sorry about the milk. Aren't you, Doris?" Nico nodded to Doris.

"I'm sorry about the milk," Doris sobbed.

"We'll all watch her, ma'am," Nico called.

Bernadette rolled up the window. The ignition caught and the truck began to hum.

Lucy pulled out her paper. What should she write?

She remembered Mama teaching Dilly to sew. If Dilly made a mistake, Dilly would pull out stiches until she got to the last perfect one, stick her needle in the cloth, and begin again. *Thank you for the ride,* Lucy scribbled. She pressed the paper against the window.

Bernadette glanced at the note, but Lucy didn't know if she read it. The truck lurched into gear. Lucy jumped back, and the truck shot forward, then picked up speed, screeching around the corner. When the roar of the motor faded, they stood watching where it had turned.

"You sure she's got a good part?" Nico asked Eugene.

"Shut up," Bald Doris said.

The street was deserted. They would have a hard time finding another ride here. How long would it take to walk to the highway?

Lucy was shoving her pencil and paper back in her pocket when she heard a car approach from the other direction. Her head popped up.

It was the truck again.

Bernadette stomped on the brakes. She cranked the window down. "If I had a brain in my head, I would keep driving."

Lucy's eyes shifted to Nico.

"You do what I say, or I will call Meany Mac and Grumpy and tell them where you are, and I won't feel one bit bad about it."

"Yes, ma'am," Eugene, Nico, and Bald Doris agreed.

Bernadette looked at Lucy, a question in her eyes.

Bald Doris stepped forward. "I got to do the talking for her. But she agrees, don't you, Lucy?"

The words came into Lucy's brain in a rush. But the shame closed her throat like a noose.

I speak for myself stayed stuck behind the cage of her teeth.

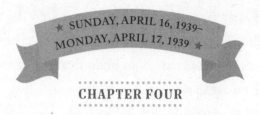

CHAPTER FOUR

"FIRST SOUND COME OUT"

Bernadette made them sit in a line on the tailgate.

"Like I told you, overnight guests will get me kicked out. I can't lose this place. No other rooming houses would take a baby. I need your word you'll do what I say." Bernadette's eyes were fixed on Bald Doris.

"Yes, ma'am." They nodded.

Bernadette chewed on her lip. "Go in the back door. Turn right. Stairwell goes up to my floor. First door on the right. One at a time. Quiet as a fox squirrel on snow. Eugene, you keep your sister in line, do you hear?"

Doris glared at Bernadette. Eugene nodded. "Yes, ma'am."

"Don't let anyone see you. My neighbors like gossip better than brown sugar crumble cake. Make their day to tell my landlady."

26

Bernadette had them lie flat in the truck bed under the feed sacks.

The truck rumbled warm under Lucy's belly. Her leg bumped against Eugene's. Nico's hair tickled her face.

The air outside grew cooler. Night was falling.

The truck swung left, then left again before coming to a stop. The cab door squeaked open, then closed.

Lucy went first, stealing down the path through the tall trees with their long twilight shadows. At the back stoop, she twisted the knob.

Somewhere someone was playing dance music. A lady laughed. The wood groaned under Lucy's feet as she climbed the stairs.

At the landing, Lucy saw Bernadette and slipped inside her room.

"Good," Bernadette whispered.

Lucy took in the praise. It filled her belly like the milk had.

The room was small and tidy. One side was stacked high with mason jars of jam, pickles, and tomatoes; another with rounds of cheese.

Lucy's mouth watered, thinking of the sweet taste of berry jam. She looked at Bernadette, a question in her eyes.

"I'm the delivery girl for five farms. It's a good job." She smiled proudly. "When my baby comes, she can ride next to me."

Lucy saw the pile of diapers tucked in the corner and the drawer fitted with blankets.

On the stairs, footsteps. A minute later, Eugene appeared, followed by Bald Doris.

Doris's eyes went straight for the food. She licked her lips.

How would they keep her from stealing?

Bernadette saw them staring at the jam. "Got it counted. Every last jar. I will know if anything's missing."

They all nodded.

"I got supper for us," Bernadette said as Nico crept into the room. He was the quietest, his feet gliding across the floor.

"Don't eat too fast, don't eat too much." Bernadette pulled a loaf of bread out of a basket and began sawing. "Your stomachs aren't used to real food." She handed each of them a thick slice.

A groan slipped out of Lucy's mouth. They all stared at her.

"First sound come out of you," Eugene whispered.

Lucy shrugged, her eyes on her bread, breathing in the sweet, yeasty smell. Stale bread hardly smelled at all. Even if Matron Mackinac found her and made her sit three days in her chair, it would be worth it for this.

Doris gobbled hers up fast. Nico ate his slow and steady, like a gentleman. Eugene took small nibbles. Lucy tore hers into little pieces and slipped them one by one into her mouth, where they melted on her tongue.

Bernadette poured them each a small jar of lemonade

with flakes of ice from the cold chest. All of them watched in stunned silence. At the orphanage, all they got was water.

The ice slivers melted on Lucy's tongue. The sweetness filled her mouth.

"How long you been at that orphanage?" Bernadette asked as she set to slicing more bread.

Lucy held five fingers in the air.

"Months?" Bernadette asked.

Lucy shook her head.

"Five *years.*" Bernadette sighed. "Lordy. You?" She pointed her knife at Eugene.

"Six years."

"Six? How old are you?"

"Thirteen." Eugene held his hand over his mouth to hide his chewing. "Ran away a few times."

"Six years is a long time," Bernadette said to Doris.

"I've only been there two years," Doris said.

"How'd that happen?"

Doris directed her thumb at Eugene. "He shared our food with the neighbor girl, so Mama sent him away. I got to stay."

Eugene fell silent, his arms pulled in on himself.

"Your mama still alive?"

Eugene and Doris nodded. A lot of the kids at the orphanage had parents who sent them away because they couldn't afford to feed them. Lucy had heard a rumor that Eugene and Doris's mama was in prison, but who knew if that was true.

"I only been there one hundred and ninety-three days," Nico offered. "But I thought about running every one of them."

Bernadette peered at Nico. "This Frank and Alice in Chicago, they kin?"

Nico shook his head.

"Do they know you're coming?"

"No," Nico mumbled.

"But they're good folks?"

Nico nodded. "No need to worry about that." His leg quivered.

"Yoo-hoo, Bernadette!" a high-pitched voice called from the stairwell.

"Shh!" Bernadette put her finger to her mouth. They listened to the heavy footsteps that climbed the stairs and the huffing, wheezing breaths.

"Mrs. Potts," Bernadette called, maneuvering her big baby stomach out the door and closing it behind her.

"Oh, honey girl, don't you look pretty." Mrs. Potts chattered between panting breaths. "Listen, dearie, I wouldn't bother you, but Mother Swanson got a call from Hannah Mackinac. Said Hannah saw you pick up some runaways."

"Yep," Bernadette said. "Took 'em down to Petrosky."

"Oh dear," Mrs. Potts huffed. "We best not get mixed up in orphanage business. You got enough on your plate with that baby coming."

"Yes, ma'am."

"Petrosky, you say. I'll let Mother Swanson know."

Lucy wondered why Mackinac was still looking for them. Grundy would go after a runaway, but no farther than Riverport. Mackinac didn't care. When kids ran off, she said "Good riddance to bad rubbish."

"Want me to bring you up a plate?" Mrs. Potts asked. "Might as well eat. You won't get one red cent off your bill if you don't."

"Thank you kindly, Mrs. Potts."

"All righty, then. You take care of yourself, dearie."

Bernadette slipped back inside, her hand resting on her large stomach, steadying herself, her green eyes traveling fast across the room.

"They're still looking for you. . . ." Bernadette peered at them. "Must have recognized me, so they knew who to call. We best change up the plan. I'll take you to Chicago myself. We'll go very early so that I can make my morning deliveries. But you got to promise you won't come back here."

They all looked at Nico.

"No need to," he whispered with authority. "Frank and Alice are city people."

Bernadette nodded, her eyes on a photo of a handsome man in an air force uniform. Bernadette's husband? Lucy hoped he was a good man who would take care of Bernadette and their baby.

* * *

The plate Mrs. Potts left outside the door was piled high with boiled potatoes, chicken, and cabbage. Bernadette handed Eugene the knife and he split it five ways. They each ate their part, taking turns with the utensils. Doris went last. When they were done, Lucy's stomach felt as full as it had ever been.

Bernadette made them a bed on the floor with pillows that were thick and soft. If you were lucky enough to have a pillow at the orphanage, it was narrow, and tough as chewed meat. Lucy shared a pillow with Nico, but it was so large, they never touched heads.

Lucy slept deeply, dreaming she was inside Bernadette's tummy, with shelves of jam jars all around.

"Time to go." Bernadette shook her. Lucy looked at the clock on the bedside table. It was four in the morning and pitch-black outside.

Eugene was already up, helping Bernadette pack cheese rounds and jam jars into crates and carrying them down to the truck.

Lucy made sure Doris got up. She helped her fold her bedding. Then they snuck down after Eugene.

"You got the address?" Bernadette asked Nico as Lucy climbed into the back.

"Yes, ma'am," Nico said.

Bernadette smiled, her tense forehead relaxing. "Good."

The truck started up and Lucy snuggled close to the others to stay warm. When she woke, hours later, the truck was stopped and Nico was climbing into the cab to give directions.

Lucy watched as they rolled by flashes of the lake, houses, train and trolley tracks. Finally, the truck came to a stop in front of a restaurant with a sign that read BOB AND BETTY'S.

Nico got out of the truck. "We're here," he said.

Lucy stared at him. Why weren't they going to Frank and Alice's house?

"They'll be here for breakfast. They come at nine," Nico answered, reading Lucy's questioning look.

Only rich people ate in restaurants. And only really rich people ate in restaurants every day.

Bernadette appeared behind Nico. "All righty, then. I'm not going to find anything missing, am I?" Bernadette looked at them, her eyes lingering on Bald Doris.

They all shook their heads.

Bernadette went down the row, shaking hands. "Good luck," she said, but when she got to Lucy, Lucy gave her a quick hug. Bernadette smiled warm as butter on biscuits. She hurried back to the cab to get a bundle tied in a dishcloth, which she handed to Lucy.

Through the gap by the knotted top, Lucy saw bread and cheese.

"Thank you, ma'am," Eugene, Bald Doris, and Nico all said.

Thank you. Lucy flashed the words on a prewritten page.

Bernadette scrambled back in the truck. The cab door slammed. The motor started up.

Wait!

The word filled Lucy's chest.

But the truck didn't come back. Bernadette was gone, just like Dilly.

January 6, 1939
Home for Friendless Children
Riverport, Iowa

Dear Sir,

I am writing to inquire into the whereabouts of my sister. Her name is Lucy Simone Sauvé. She is eleven years old. She has blue eyes, red curly hair & a way of looking at you that you won't forget real easy.

I'm 17 & I have a job. I make enough money to take care of my sister and myself. Lucy is the only family I have left. Please could you let me know if she is there.

Yours truly,
Dilly Sauvé

P.S. The envelope inside is private to Lucy Simone Sauvé. Please give it to her right away.

January 6, 1939
Home for Friendless Children
Riverport, Iowa

Dear Lucy,

I can't believe I'm writing words you will read.
There are so many things all up in my brain I want to
tell you & I don't know where to start.

Every day I wonder what you think about what
happened. I can't imagine how sad you must be that
I haven't ever written to you. Please know how hard
I've tried to find you. I didn't know where you were
until today, when I came home from Mrs. LaFinestre's
shop & Mrs. Sokoloff handed me a letter from Mama.
My legs stopped holding me up right then.

The date on the envelope postmark was January 2,
1939, but the date on the letter was March 3, 1934!
I found a note on the back of the envelope from the
maid at the Riverport house where Mama had worked.
She said Mama's letter had slipped behind an old
dresser and nobody knew it was there.

The letter was sent to the address where the
Sokoloffs used to live. Remember the bachelors who
lived below us? The tall bachelor saw it and brought it
to Mrs. Sokoloff.

The letter said where you were at! I'm so excited

that my handwriting has gone wobbly and I don't
think I will sleep at all tonight.

I will send $$ for a train ticket & you will come to
live with me and the Sokoloffs. I have put an envelope
with stamps on it addressed to us. Please write as soon
as you can!!! I can't wait to hear!

Love,

Dilly

P.S. I forgot to say, I live in the Sokoloffs' daughter's
home with Mr. and Mrs. Sokoloff, their daughter, and
her husband and three children. They have been good
to me, but it isn't home. Home is you and Mama and
me. Now it is just you and me.

CHAPTER FIVE

THE SMELL OF FRYING BACON

They sat down on the cold curb to wait for Frank and Alice.

Lucy brought out her paper and wrote, *My sister lives in Chicago.*

Doris peered over Lucy's shoulder. "She's lying. She doesn't have anyone."

"Shut up, Doris," Eugene said.

Nico's eyes softened. "Do you know where she lives?"

Lucy shook her head.

"Did she send you letters?"

Lucy cast her eyes down.

Nico nodded. "Once we get settled in with Frank and Alice, we'll look for her," he said.

First move in to Frank and Alice's, then find Dilly. Nico's answer was sensible. It felt right.

Lucy settled back to watch the waitresses in pink uniforms carry stacks of pancakes and pots of hot coffee. The smell of frying bacon wafted out the door.

After a while, Lucy untied the dish towel and handed out Bernadette's food. It was less than Lucy had expected. She grew hungrier after they ate, knowing there was nothing more.

Every few minutes, someone would check the time on a nearby bank building. It was seven, seven-thirty, eight, nine, then nine-thirty.

Nico's foot had begun to fidget like crazy. "Stay here! I'll be back," he said, sauntering into the diner, where he turned a corner by the booths and disappeared.

Why had he gone in? Had he seen Frank and Alice?

They pressed their faces to the window, waiting.

Lucy tried to calm herself by thinking of things Frank and Alice would like about her. She was a great reader. She was good at math. She was a good speller. She took her list of vocabulary words out and tested herself. She knew them all.

"Nobody's going to give you a vocabulary test now!" Bald Doris barked.

Lucy folded up the list and put it in her pocket.

Bald Doris stalked the windows.

Eugene returned to the curb. He pulled a ball of rubber bands out of his pocket and began tossing it in the air while keeping one eye on the door. Lucy sat down next to him. When she looked back, Doris had disappeared.

Lucy tapped Eugene's arm and pointed to where Doris had been.

Eugene nodded, but didn't get up.

Lucy wiggled her paper out of her pocket and wrote, *Should we go in?* But before Eugene could answer, Nico, Bald Doris, a tall man with dark hair and a fancy suit, a beautiful blond woman in blue, and a little boy of five or six all dressed up like a man came walking toward the register.

It was Frank and Alice. It had to be.

Lucy and Eugene jumped up and rushed the door.

Bald Doris gripped one of Frank's hands. The young boy in the grown-up clothes held the other. The little boy let go when Frank got to the register to pay. Bald Doris did not.

Alice wore a cinched-waist suit and a hat with a feather. Lucy smiled at her like the kind of girl you would want to have around, but Alice didn't notice her.

Lucy tried to read Nico's face. His expression was calm, but one hand was gripping the other so tightly it was white around his fingers, and his leg was jiggling.

Frank was laughing with the man behind the register. He bought a pack of cigarettes and gave them to Alice. They all came outside, blinking in the bright sunshine.

"Isn't Frank handsome?" Bald Doris asked.

Lucy nodded. He and Alice were as beautiful as characters on a book cover, but she didn't know if you were supposed to say that out loud.

"So this must be Eugene and Lucy," Frank said.

Lucy smiled. Frank knew her name!

Frank shook Eugene's hand, then Lucy's. Lucy liked the sure way his fingers gripped hers.

Lucy took in Frank's smile, the stylish hat, and the soft overcoat. He was more handsome and better dressed than Lucy had imagined. The young boy wore a tailored coat with the collar pulled up and a hat like Frank's.

Lucy imagined going back to the orphanage all dressed up. That would be something.

"Nico has always had a gift for making friends." Frank nodded to Lucy and Eugene.

Nico nodded stiffly.

Lucy liked Frank's kind voice and how nice he was to Nico. He cared about him. She watched Alice sink her painted fingernails into white gloves.

Lucy's rapid breathing began to slow. Her stiff face relaxed.

"We shared some good times with Nico, didn't we, Alice?"

Alice nodded.

How could Lucy make Frank and Alice care about her the way they cared about Nico?

Frank pulled a vial out of his pocket and poured a drop of clear liquid on the pad of each fingertip. He passed his fingers through his hair and set his hat back on his head, checking his reflection in the window. Then he took out his handkerchief and wiped each of his fingers.

When he was finished, Frank turned his attention to Nico. "Thanks for looking us up, buddy." He cuffed Nico's head playfully.

Lucy tried to make eye contact with Alice. But Alice was busy lighting a cigarette. Frank's arm returned to his side and the little boy grabbed it. Lucy ached to hold Frank's hand the way the boy did.

But what was wrong with Nico? His lips were smiling, but his eyes looked like he was waiting to be whacked with Mackinac's belt.

"Nice to meet you all. Thanks for stopping by." Frank bowed, and he and Alice and the little boy began walking away.

What? Where were they going?

Bald Doris planted her feet in front of Frank. "We didn't stop by. We came to live with you."

Nico sent Bald Doris a withering look.

Frank nodded. "And as I explained, lovely girl, that is most flattering. We only wish it could happen, don't we, Alice?"

"It can happen. Don't you see?" Bald Doris pointed out.

"We appreciate the difficulty of your situation." Frank frowned. "But I'm afraid we are on our way to Grand Rapids for an important engagement. We bid you Godspeed in your travels, don't we, Willy?"

The little boy nodded, tightening his grip on Frank's hand.

"How about just me? Can I come along?" Doris offered.

"We would take you if we could, my lady. But we only

have three tickets." Frank pressed his lips together and shook his head.

"You could buy more," Bald Doris suggested.

"I wish." Frank clucked. "I'm afraid we have to be going or we'll miss our train."

Alice and Willy began walking again. Frank hurried to catch up.

A lady coming out of the diner stopped to stare at Frank, Alice, and Willy. The three of them were dazzling.

Lucy's worn-out dress was gray from years of washing in the same basin. Doris's dress was too small. Eugene's pants too large. Nico's only had one belt loop and his shirt was patched.

They looked pathetic.

"Like I always say, buddy," Frank called back to Nico, "nothing lasts forever."

Nico took a deep, shaky breath. "It was nice to see you again, Frank, Alice," he mumbled in a small voice.

"There's my boy." Frank tipped his hat at Nico.

"Frank! Frank!" Bald Doris ran in front of Frank and waved her hand in his face. "I know. . . . I could take care of Willy."

"Oh no. We wouldn't dream of using your talents as a mere nanny, my dear girl. You are destined for greatness," Frank told Doris, veering around her. He, Alice, and Willy walked faster.

Bald Doris grabbed Frank's coat. "You don't understand. I want to!"

Frank froze. "Don't touch the coat," he growled.

Bald Doris released his sleeve but continued to chase him. Nico did not move. Lucy stood next to him and Eugene.

When Frank, Alice, Willy, and Bald Doris disappeared around the corner, Nico crumpled in a heap on the curb, his leg finally still.

This couldn't be happening. Frank and Alice would be back, wouldn't they?

Nico had been so sure.

"We're better off without them," Eugene said with a trembling voice.

"No, we're not," Nico whispered.

Lucy could see how Frank and Alice might not want to take them all. But why would they leave Nico?

Bald Doris came skipping back. "Look what I got." She clutched a dollar bill between two grimy fingers. "Frank paid me to go away." She grinned.

Lucy knew she should be glad about this. A dollar was an awful lot of money. But her chest felt hollow and her hands colder than they'd ever been before.

CHAPTER SIX

"FIRECRACKER SMART"

Lucy could feel the dark water of hopelessness rise inside her. She knew the sensation all too well. Miss Holland and Matron Mackinac had made her feel that way. Try as she might, she couldn't get their voices out of her head.

What is the matter with you, you useless girl?

But she'd figured out what to do about them. She'd stopped talking, and then she'd run away. Now she would never have to see Miss Holland, Matron Mackinac, or Matron Grundy again.

Eugene stood by the restaurant door as if Frank and Alice were still inside. Nico sat slumped on the curb, his head in his hands. Lucy pressed her page against the restaurant window and wrote:

Why didn't Frank and Alice want Nico?

Eugene shrugged. "Replaced him," he murmured.

With Willy?

Eugene nodded. "Nico got too old. He says Frank and Alice like kids who are firecracker smart but look young and innocent. No poker players suspect a little kid would peek at a man's cards and report what he saw to Frank. That's what Nico did for Frank and I guess it's what Willy does now."

Lucy nodded. So Frank cheated. That was how he got rich.

Eugene ran his finger along the glass. "He was never going to take all of us anyway."

Lucy didn't think Eugene had believed this. Still, it felt good to hear him say it.

Now for sure Lucy would find Dilly. But what if Dilly had a new family and a new sister? What if Lucy had been traded for someone else just like Nico had? She thought about the way Dilly laughed. And how she had sewn a doll out of polka-dotted and striped fabric scraps. She had glued the yarn hair in red ringlets just like Lucy's and Mama's and her own. She'd fashioned wire-rimmed glasses that she'd sewn to the sides of the doll's head.

The doll had three button eyes and one button nose, so Lucy had named her Mrs. Three Eyes. But Mrs. Three Eyes had been orphan-borrowed the first night at the Home for Friendless Children. Lucy reached in her pocket for the blue button that had been the doll's nose. She had found it on the floor next to her bed and carried it with her ever since.

Lucy sat down next to Nico. She'd tell him her plan to

find Dilly. If Dilly was still living with the Sokoloffs, they might take Lucy in. But what about Nico, Eugene, and Bald Doris? The Sokoloffs' apartment had been small.

"I'm getting candy," Doris announced, swinging the diner door back and forth.

Lucy shook her head. They would need that dollar.

Bald Doris pushed forward into the line at the cash register behind a big lady in a yellow dress.

Nico still had not moved. Lucy tapped his arm, but he ignored her.

In school when there was a problem Lucy couldn't solve, she would write down all her possible choices. It was comforting to see things on paper, easier to decide what to do. She turned her page over to where there was a big clear spot. She did not want to spend time erasing now.

But wait.

Someone had written on her paper.

Lucy looked closer.

If Frank and Alice don't work out, call Jabo KAR-0421, it said.

Who could have written that?

CHAPTER SEVEN

A LIE THEY TOLD ORPHANS

Eugene wouldn't write on Lucy's paper. It wasn't Bald Doris's handwriting. And it would never have occurred to Nico that Frank and Alice wouldn't work out.

Bernadette? She must have written on the paper after Lucy had fallen asleep.

Lucy showed Eugene.

He let out a tense breath. "Bernadette," he whispered.

Lucy nodded.

"That's a phone number?" Eugene asked.

Lucy pointed to the diner, where a phone hung near the register.

"Nico knows the guy behind the counter. He should be the one to ask," Eugene said. He drew closer to Nico. "We need your help. We got someone better than Frank and Alice."

Nico wheezed, wiping his nose with the back of his hand. "No one better," he said.

Eugene snorted. "Nico, they left us here with nothing."

Nico didn't respond.

Eugene sighed. "Think the restaurant guy will let you use his phone?"

"I dunno," Nico mumbled.

Lucy tapped Nico's arm, then set the paper in his lap. She watched his eyes move across it.

"What do I say when this Jabo guy answers?" Nico asked.

Bernadette told you to call, Lucy wrote as fast as she could.

"Right," Eugene said.

Nico blew his nose on his sleeve and ran his hands through his hair. He rolled his shoulders back, slipping on his old confidence. He strode into the busy diner and approached the man behind the counter.

"What's he doing?" Bald Doris asked, one hand in her candy bag.

"He's calling a friend of Bernadette's." Eugene spoke fast, his voice pitched high. "She wrote someone's name on Lucy's paper. Said we should call him if we needed help. You gonna share?"

Doris pulled out a big piece of licorice and stuffed it in her mouth. "I earned it, not you."

Eugene glared at her.

She rolled her eyes, then dug in her bag for a tiny piece.

Eugene split it in three, which wasn't easy, given how small it was.

Nico's skin was blotchy and his nose red, but he was smiling when he came out.

They all clamored around him. "What did he say?" Doris and Eugene asked.

"Bob said I could use the phone so long as we didn't hang around here anymore. Jabo said he'd be here in an hour."

"Did he sound nice?" Eugene asked.

Nico nodded.

It had been a long time since Lucy had known a nice adult. Miss Ellie, the teacher, had been nice. All the girls cried when Miss Ellie left. Bernadette had been nice, but she was so young. The meanness of adulthood hadn't taken over yet.

Eugene hitched up his pants. "Where are we supposed to meet him?"

"Down the road a bit," Nico said.

Lucy hoped Jabo lived close by. She didn't want to get too far from Chicago.

"That's crazy." Bald Doris crossed her arms. "I'm not going to wait for some guy we don't even know."

"He's a friend of Bernadette's," Nico said.

"I didn't like Bernadette. She didn't let us stay with her," Bald Doris said.

"It was against the rules of her rooming house," Nico said.

Bald Doris rolled her eyes. "She could have figured it out. And she could have given us more food. Did you see how much she had?"

Nico snorted. "You're just mad because she bawled you out."

"Am not," Bald Doris said. "But I'm not waiting for a stranger to pick us up and take us who knows where. Eugene and I are going back to the orphanage."

"Nope." Eugene said the word hard, like a doorstop.

"Well, I am." Doris flounced away.

Lucy wasn't going back to the orphanage. Not ever.

Once they got established at Jabo's, she would find Dilly.

The diner guy with the bald head came out. He threw a mean look their way, then made a big show of cleaning their fingerprints off the glass door.

"Let's go," Nico said under his breath.

They started walking to the spot where Jabo had said he'd pick them up. Bald Doris trailed behind, her lips black with licorice.

When Lucy looked back, Doris made a face and said, "This is the way to the orphanage, too."

Maybe it would be good if Bald Doris went back. Bernadette had said they wouldn't make it with her along.

They walked by a shop that sold snuff and a barber school with haircuts for ten cents. Who had the money to pay for a haircut? Rich people or people who didn't own scissors.

When they passed an apartment building with a crisscross

of clotheslines, Lucy felt a sharp stab of homesickness, remembering the time Dilly had reeled in their bachelor neighbor's undershirt by mistake and had to knock on his door to return it.

But except for the clotheslines, this place was not familiar. Lucy searched the faces they passed. Strangers.

When Nico announced they were at the meeting place, they found a small patch of grass to settle on and wait.

"I'm not doing this," Bald Doris announced. She marched across the street and stuck out her thumb.

The cars whizzed by. When one slowed to pick her up, Doris ran back to them. She plunked herself down and ate every last piece of candy.

A few minutes later, she threw up a pool of black licorice barf. Then she cleaned herself up and sat down, facing away from the others.

At the orphanage you were taught to forget about the bad things. Your life *before* was over. But that was a lie they told orphans. Lucy knew regular people celebrated birthdays and anniversaries. Regular people took photographs and kept diaries. Regular people had things they loved for their whole entire lives. Regular people remembered.

Of course there were things Lucy wished she could forget, but most of them had happened at the orphanage. And that was all over now. She'd never be humiliated like that again.

It was warm at first, but then gray clouds moved in and a cold wind came up. Each time a car rolled by, they jumped up.

"I told you we shouldn't wait for him. No one ever listens to me," Bald Doris grumbled after more cars sped by.

Lucy trusted Bernadette. Bernadette wouldn't tell them to call someone who was mean.

"It's him!" Nico shouted when a brightly painted truck with fancy scrolls around the cab pulled off the road.

Lucy jumped to get a glimpse of the driver, but she could see no one.

The tires squealed as the truck came to a halt. They all ran to the driver's side, which didn't have a door.

The driver was a tiny man perched on a throne of cushions.

But there was something strange about him. The man had no head.

PART TWO

CHAPTER EIGHT

"ENCYCLOPEDIA OF THE INCREDIBLE"

The man's hand clutched a cigar.

Lucy took a step closer. If you don't have a mouth, she wondered, how do you smoke?

The cigar hand moved to the shirt and stuck the cigar in the gap between two buttons.

His mouth was in his chest?

A deep voice boomed out of his shirt. "Hey, what do you think of my cranium?" He reached over to the passenger seat for his head, which he dangled by the hair for her to see.

Bald Doris shrieked.

"Nice," Nico said, his voice calm.

The head looked as if it was made of ladies' stockings stuffed with rags. The hair was sewn on, the nose was lumpy, but the eyes were startlingly real.

Then Lucy noticed there were holes in the man's shirt with eyes looking through. A short arm reached up to a headless collar. With three buttons unfastened, the man's real head popped out.

He was middle-aged, with a high forehead, a receding hairline, and folds of skin around his mouth.

" 'Bout wet myself," Eugene admitted.

The driver's smile was warm. "I'm sorry to have frightened you"—he bowed to Eugene—"but I've run out of the gullible, the credulous, and the unsuspecting. I'm trying out for ringmaster. I will need quite the arsenal of tricks to get that coveted spot."

"Ringmaster? You're in a circus?" Eugene asked.

Jabo nodded.

"Do you even need an act? As small as you are, isn't that enough . . ." Nico's voice trailed off.

"Size is an accident of birth, my fine sir. The secret to showmanship is invention. A short person has to do twice the work to be considered half as good, so yes indeed, I must have many tricks up my sleeve."

He passed the head down for them to inspect.

"The eyes are really good," Nico told him.

He nodded. "Made of glass. I sent to Philadelphia for them. Still working on the mouth. I'm considering facial hair."

Bald Doris butted in front of Eugene. "A beard," she announced, though she did not touch the head when it was offered to her.

The driver nodded, taking back his head and placing it tenderly on the seat. "I'm Jabo, and you must be Doris, Eugene, Lucy, and Nico." He bowed to each of them. "The pleasure is all mine."

"How'd you know our names?" Nico asked.

"Bernadette gave me a comprehensive report," Jabo said.

"My hair is growing back. Did Bernadette tell you that?" Bald Doris leaned her head down to show him.

"Indeed." Jabo nodded to Doris, who smiled, pleased with herself.

Jabo jumped from the seat to the running board and pulled a crank. With a *thrunk,* a row of steps appeared from under the chassis and he walked down.

He wore black-and-white-checkered trousers, a bright blue jacket, yellow socks, and red shoes. On the ground, he barely came up to Lucy's chest, and she was the second-smallest eleven-year-old at the orphanage.

Jabo took a deep bow. "What you see here is a sample of the driver. The full driver will come later."

Lucy popped her hand over her mouth to keep the laugh inside.

"Let it out, my girl," Jabo said. "Laughter is popcorn for the soul. Now, I have inquiries for you, and I expect you have been formulating questions for me."

Nico's fingers raked his hair. "Mr. Jabo, sir, on the phone you said you would help us."

"Allow me to elaborate. . . . You will be given excellent

cuisine and a warm, safe place to sleep, until the show goes on the rails on Sunday. After that, it will be up to you."

"What will be up to us?" Doris asked, her eyes tracking him as he walked stiffly back and forth.

"Your food and lodging. I'm hoping you will find someone to sponsor you, an apprenticeship arrangement . . . in which case, the situation will be permanent." He stuck his finger in the air. "I wish I could offer you more time, but no one will remain in Winter Quarters after we jump to our first stand. We are a rail show, after all."

"What's a rail show?" Nico asked.

"A circus that moves by train from performance spot to performance spot, known in circus parlance as a stand."

"We're going to the circus?" Doris asked.

"Indeed. The circus is home. I hope Saachi's will be family for you, too."

"Will it perform in Chicago?" Nico asked.

"The first week in May, if I'm not mistaken. I should also mention that in your quest for an apprenticeship, you will be allowed three mistakes—errors in judgment, if you will."

"Mistakes?" Nico frowned.

Jabo nodded. "Yes. Ah, so much to explain. Lucy, would you climb in the cab, there?" He pointed a wobbly finger to the truck. "On the floor well of the passenger seat is a black velvet box. Could you bring it down to me, please?"

Jabo had picked her!

Lucy hurried to the truck, which smelled of peppermint

and cigar smoke. A basket of books was on the floor. Her breathing quickened. . . . Jabo owned books!

Under the basket, she spotted a black velvet box the size of a serving platter. She worked the box out from under the books and climbed down the stairs, carrying it as if it were as precious as a dictionary.

Jabo searched their faces. "Anybody have a bugle? A trumpet or a kazoo would do."

They all shook their heads.

"Well, then . . . a drumroll will suffice." He leaned down and drummed his legs with his hands. Then he took the box from Lucy, lifted the black velvet lid, and peeked inside.

The box was divided into many square velvet-lined compartments filled with small objects like shiny pebbles, feathers, and dice.

Jabo walked around, peering up at them.

"This is only a guess of where you might fit in at Saachi's. It is based on my observations and Bernadette's insights. Don't be afraid to prove me off the beam, wide of the mark, otherwise known as incorrect. Only you can feel the tick of your own heart from the inside. Now . . . ladies first."

Jabo stuck his hand in the box and walked toward Lucy. When his fingers uncurled, there on the flat of his palm was a tiny silk blue-striped pouch. Lucy loosened the delicate ribbon drawstring and pulled out three black hairs, each about five inches in length.

"Hair?" Nico asked.

Jabo smiled. "Three pachyderm tail hairs, to be exact."

"What's a pachyderm?" Doris asked.

"An elephant," Jabo answered.

The hairs were strong, and black as burnt toast. Lucy let her fingers explore the length of them. She offered the bristly hairs for the others to touch, then wound them in a loose circle and slipped them back inside the pouch.

Thank you. Lucy showed her page to Jabo. She loved the little silk drawstring bag but was not quite sure what to make of the elephant hairs.

"I'm the one who needs hair, not her," Doris groused.

"Patience, Mademoiselle Doris. You are next." Jabo began the drumroll again. Then he walked toward Doris and opened his fingers.

In his hand were two red balls, each the size of a wrist pincushion. They were flat on one side, round on the other. The flat side had a triangular hollow.

Eugene took one of the red balls and pressed it against his nose. His hand dropped. The ball stayed on.

Everybody laughed.

Doris put the other nose on and grinned. Eugene handed Nico a nose to try.

"But how come Lucy got three and I only got two?" Doris asked.

"A shrewd observation, Mademoiselle Doris," Jabo said.

"Does that mean she only gets two chances?" Nico chimed in.

"Very good, Nico. Yes, I'm afraid Doris has used one of her chances already."

"That's not possible. I only just met you. It's because of my hair, isn't it?"

Jabo's head waggled. "I believe you've made an error in judgment of the aspirational variety. In other words, I'm guessing the hair situation is tangentially related."

Bald Doris frowned. "What's that supposed to mean?"

One of Jabo's short fingers popped into the air. "I feel a tooth riddle coming on. . . ."

Lucy pulled the baby tooth from her pocket and held it out so Jabo could see.

"A kindred spirit!" Jabo winked at her. "Now my riddle. What has many teeth and sings its own song?"

"A singer," Doris said.

"Good answer, but incorrect," Jabo said.

"Bernadette?" Eugene suggested.

"You are getting warmer, in a manner of speaking, sir."

Who was close to Bernadette? The baby in her tummy? The neighbor lady, Mrs. Potts? But Lucy didn't know what either of them looked like. And she certainly had no idea about their teeth.

Lucy took out her page and wrote *aspirational.* The root word was *aspire,* which meant something you wanted. What did Bald Doris want?

Hair, of course, but hair didn't have teeth and it didn't sing. Wait . . . what about a comb? A comb had teeth and it could make music. A girl at the orphanage had played "Jingle Bells" on her comb. *Comb?* Lucy wrote.

"Excellent!" Jabo thundered.

Lucy grinned. But what did this have to do with why Bald Doris had only two chances?

Jabo fixed Doris with a penetrating look. "That is correct . . . is it not, Mademoiselle Doris?"

How would Doris know if the answer was correct?

Doris's eye twitched. She scratched at her head. "I don't know what you're talking about," she said.

"I believe you've made a one-chance mistake. I would not allow it to increase in size—mushroom, if you will—to a two-chance mistake," Jabo said softly.

Bald Doris wheeled around and stuck her hand deep in her dress. When she turned back, she had a silver comb in her palm.

Jabo took the comb and ran a finger over the engraved *B*. "Common courtesy is a somewhat uncommon commodity, I'm afraid. I will make certain Bernadette gets her comb back."

Doris scowled. "Now do I get my third chance?"

"I imagine you know the answer to that question," Jabo said under his breath.

"No, I don't," Bald Doris insisted, spit flying out of her mouth.

"That would be correct." Jabo nodded.

Doris crossed her arms. "I meant no, I don't know the answer."

"And now you do." Jabo bowed with a great flourish. "Now Eugene . . ." Jabo began the drumroll again. Out of the box he pulled three playing cards: an ace of hearts, an ace of diamonds, and an ace of clubs. On the back of each was an elaborate picture of a monkey playing a violin.

"An ace is a powerful card," Jabo explained. "You may have heard the expression 'an ace in the hole,' which means something hidden that can provide a sure victory. That is how we see you, my steadfast friend."

"Thank you, sir." Eugene's eyes were on the ground, but his smile had an intensity Lucy hadn't seen before.

"You're welcome." Jabo nodded. "And last but not least, Nico."

After the drumroll, Jabo poked around in the box until he pulled out what looked like three black caterpillars: one bushy, one curly, one sleek. Nico inspected them for a long time; then he took one of the black furry shapes and placed it above his upper lip. It stuck.

"Correct!" Jabo cried.

Soon they were all trying them on. Doris looked hilarious in the curly mustache. Eugene took on the air of a middle-aged man in the bushy one. Nico looked the best in the sleek mustache.

"Thank you." Nico imitated Jabo's showman's bow, then asked, "So, how do you know Bernadette?"

Good question, Lucy thought.

"We are both members of O-O-F-O, pronounced '*ooooof-oh*.' The Order of Fine Orphans. OOFOs look out for other orphans."

"You were an orphan?" Eugene asked.

"In a manner of speaking," Jabo said.

Nico nodded. "So . . . we have a week to get an apprenticeship, and we can each make three mistakes, except Doris only gets two because she already made one."

"Precisely and concisely," Jabo said.

"But exactly what kind of apprenticeships are available?" Eugene asked.

" 'Available' "—Jabo rubbed his neck, then pulled up his jacket sleeve to check one of three wristwatches—"may be a somewhat misleading characterization of the apprenticeship experience. But let's not concern ourselves with the details just yet. We're behind schedule here. Your chariot awaits." He waved to the back of the truck.

"Where are we going?" Doris asked.

"Winter Quarters."

Nico eyed the dummy head and said, "Headless Headquarters?"

"You are a clever one, Nico, but no. Headquarters of the great, the one and only Saachi's Circus Spectacular. An encyclopedia of the incredible, if you will."

Jabo sank back on his heels.

"Now one last question . . . do you know why Mrs.

Mackinac and Mrs. Grundy of the home—I use the term with all due irony—have such an uncommon interest in you?"

They all shook their heads.

"Of course, they don't like runaways. But once the infraction has occurred, they aren't likely to pursue perpetrators beyond the boundaries of Riverport. And yet Bernadette reported today they were combing Dinton and Blaneville with unusual fervor."

He searched their eyes, settling on Bald Doris.

"Mademoiselle Doris?"

Doris poked her chin out. "How should I know?" she muttered.

Jabo nodded thoughtfully, then pivoted on his small feet.

"When Bernadette left the orphanage, did she go to your circus?" Eugene wanted to know.

"Yes, my fine sir. But alas, Bernadette does not have sawdust in her shoes."

"Sir?" Nico asked.

"It means she isn't cut out for circus life. Our loss, I'm afraid. All righty, then, we must be going." He nodded toward the back of the truck and they piled in. "In the circus, timing is everything. It pounds through the place like a blood flow. Arriving after the cook tent flag has gone down is a tragedy indeed. I've seen grown men ford across snake-infested rivers for Nitty-Bitty's fried chicken and corn fritters."

Lucy smiled. She liked Jabo so much, she would go

anywhere he went. She just hoped Winter Quarters wasn't too far from Chicago.

Though she did wonder why the circus hadn't been right for Bernadette and what Jabo would consider a mistake. Stealing, clearly. But what else?

Jabo hadn't asked about her silence. He had accepted this part of her. She would not lose a chance for this.

Lucy brought her knees up and held them tightly against her chest as the truck rolled forward. She picked at the worn threads of her stockings until she'd made a hole, and then she tried to weave the threads back together so no one would see.

"THE WORLD'S SMALLEST MAN MEETS THE WORLD'S LARGEST DOG."

Jabo drove slower than Bernadette and pushed the accelerator, then the brakes, in fits and starts. It was because he couldn't reach the gas pedal. He drove by operating poles with empty shoes attached to the bottom.

Lucy ran her fingers along the ribbon drawstring that closed the striped silk pouch. The pouch was the best part of the gift. It gave her a fourth special thing. No one else had four.

The pouch reminded her of how Dilly had made a tiny purse for Mrs. Three Eyes and sewn it to the doll's hand so Lucy wouldn't lose it.

Lucy had been so upset when Mrs. Three Eyes had been stolen. She'd searched the dorms and confronted the most notorious orphan thieves. When she still couldn't find Mrs. Three Eyes, she'd asked Mackinac for help. Mackinac had given her a kind smile and patted her head. "It's all for the best. Girls who let go of their old lives and fully commit to their new circumstances thrive here at the home. . . ."

Lucy dug in her pocket for the button. She had kept it safe, just as she would keep Jabo's gift safe.

But why had Jabo chosen to give Lucy elephant-tail hairs? She understood the ace in the hole for Eugene. He was a helpful guy. And the mustaches for Nico seemed right. Nico had the manners of a grown man. But Lucy had never seen an elephant, and she didn't understand the clown noses for Doris.

"Why'd you pinch a comb anyway?" Nico shouted to Doris over the roar of a passing truck. "You don't even have hair."

Doris frowned. "I will soon enough."

"If you live that long," Nico said.

"What's that supposed to mean?" Doris shouted.

Nico shrugged.

"At least I wasn't replaced by a six-year-old," Doris said.

Nico turned away. "I wasn't replaced," he mumbled as they rolled by a large barn and silo.

Doris snorted. "Yeah, you were."

Doris was mad about getting only two chances. She was looking for somebody to take it out on.

"Stop it." Eugene jabbed Doris's arm. "You sound like Mama."

"He started it," Doris grumbled as the farmland flew by. Small green plants in straight rows, one after another after another.

Eugene whispered something to Doris that Lucy couldn't hear.

"Did you see that comb? It was worth a lot. I was going to sell it," Doris replied.

"But why would you want to steal from her?" Eugene asked. "Bernadette was nice."

"She was the one who had it," Doris said.

Nico rolled his eyes.

The truck shimmied as it picked up speed. Lucy took out her pencil, rested the page on her knee, and wrote, *Apprenticeship?*

Dilly had been learning to be a dressmaker from Mama. That was an apprenticeship, wasn't it?

Mama had worked her way up from finisher. Dressmakers made more money and were difficult to replace. When Lucy was little, Mama had said she would teach her dressmaking, too. But Lucy didn't think she'd ever sew as well as Dilly.

Lucy handed her page to Nico, who shrugged.

Jabo? Lucy wrote.

Doris peeked over to see what Lucy was writing. She jabbed her finger at Lucy's page. "I don't like him."

"I do," Eugene said.

Nico stroked his mustaches. "Me too."

"I didn't believe that goof-oh stuff," Doris said. "Who would tell another person you're an orphan?"

Doris had a point there. Being an orphan was something to hide.

It was growing dark, how far had they come?

Headlights flashed as cars drove by. *Rat-tat-tat, rat-tat-tat,* the tires sounded as they rolled over the metal bridge slats. Lucy inched her way to the truck bed's wood side to get a better view of where they were headed.

The truck lights flashed on signs by the side of the road.

WATCH THE GREAT DIAVOLO'S DUEL WITH DEATH

SEE AMERICA'S STRONGEST WOMAN SERVE TEA WHILE CARRYING THREE ADULTS ON HER BACK

MEET ELEPHANTOFF, THE WORLD'S ONLY PARISIAN PACHYDERM HAIRDRESSER

In the orphanage classroom there was an old dictionary missing a chunk of the *R*s and all of the *S*s. Lucy wished she had it. Even when she understood the words, she liked to look them up. The definitions carved a clearer meaning in her head.

The truck swayed as it crested a small hill.

Below was a city of glittering lights. As the truck sped down to the valley, all the orphans craned their necks to see. Soon they passed a row of flags snapping from tall poles and a banner that said SAACHI'S CIRCUS SPECTACULAR.

Jabo turned in to a parking lot, tires crunching gravel. He pulled up next to an elaborately painted wagon with a piano keyboard and a giant horn.

The truck shuddered as it turned off. *Thrunk,* the stairs came down. In the distance a trumpet and a saxophone played.

Lucy's leg cramped as she climbed over the tailgate. Nico and Eugene leapt over. Bald Doris waited until Eugene opened it for her.

"Due to the short notice," Jabo said, "I haven't yet received permission for your visit. This necessitates a clandestine entrance. Please be respectful. Do not stare at the Zebra Lady's stripes. Yes, they are permanent. Do not ask the Chicken Man why he never takes off his chicken suit. That is his choice. Do not say 'How's the weather up there?' to the tall person. Or 'I could put you in my pocket' to a person of short stature."

Jabo walked fast, but his steps seemed to pain him. A thick carpet of pink wood shavings covered the ground, muffling their footsteps.

Lucy couldn't take her eyes off the large posters on the tents. There were gorillas playing baseball, fortune-telling ponies, a carriage drawn by zebras, and a man walking a tightrope between two church steeples.

The air smelled of grain, newly cut wood, and hot fry grease. From somewhere in the distance came the familiar whir of sewing machines.

In a clearing between tents, a bright light shone on two jugglers spinning balls through the air and a barely dressed blond girl doing backflips.

Through the flap door of another tent, Lucy saw people eating at picnic tables with red-and-white-checkered tablecloths. The smell of garlic and butter made her stomach grumble.

Jabo hurried them past the tents to the horse corrals, where the sawdust turned to rutted ground. The horses trotted back and forth along the corral line as they walked past. A small blacksmith shop came next, followed by three unattached railroad cars. The center car had an awning and the name J. JABO on a brass sign. Jabo climbed the mini stairs easily, but Eugene had trouble finding room for his big feet.

A pony-size dog with a black-and-white-spotted head appeared in the entrance, his long thin tail whapping the door. Jabo reached up to pet him.

"Good evening, Tiny," he said, nodding to Lucy. "The world's smallest man meets the world's largest dog. One of my best ideas, I don't mind saying. Diavolo has a million-dollar insurance policy against me growing."

Growing? He was a grown-up!

Jabo used a long stick with a carved handle to reach the light, which washed the train car in a yellow glow.

The shelves were hung low and packed with clocks and what looked like clock repair tools covered a workbench. A sign read J. JABO: WATCH REPAIR. In the back were a bed and a shelf that sagged with the weight of books.

Jabo fished in his pocket for his change and dropped it and his keys on the table. "Welcome to my humble abode. Make yourselves at home while I run down to the cook tent to sweet-talk Nitty-Bitty and procure your supper. If you see Grace, tell her you're OOFOs," he called over his shoulder as he went out.

"Who's Grace?" Nico asked, but Jabo was already gone.

Tiny circled in the same spot a few times before lying down. It shook the whole train car.

Lucy discovered Tiny liked to be scratched behind his ears. He kicked over on his back, groaning happily, his gigantic rib cage in the air, his pie-size paws flapping, his big sloppy pink-and-black-speckled jowls hanging upside down.

Doris kept her distance from the dog as she inspected Jabo's things. She picked up a gold pocket watch and examined it closely.

Uh-oh.

"I can look, can't I?" Doris snapped when she saw Lucy staring.

Nico set a tall black top hat on his head and squatted to observe himself in a mirror, hung low, the way everything was in Jabo's home.

Lucy ran her fingers along the book spines. *The Patchwork Girl of Oz, Adventures of Huckleberry Finn,* and *Paradise Lost.* Then she spotted an elaborately decorated map: *Saachi's Circus Spectacular WINTER QUARTERS, Karaboo 1939.*

On the map were roaring tigers, women with snakes wrapped around their necks like scarves, men in red coats playing trumpets, acrobats hanging by their hair, and buildings with names like Ring Stock Barn, Menagerie, Costume Shop. She spotted the elephant house and was trying to locate Jabo's train car when she heard someone on the stairs. Tiny jumped up, shaking the car, and an enormous woman wearing a plaid flannel shirt appeared. Her head and shoulders filled the doorway, though her feet stood on the ground outside.

She was wearing men's dungarees, but there was something

elegant about her. Her eyes were the green of new spring leaves. She had long, dark, shiny hair and skin as perfect as a bar of soap. She was dainty and large at the same time.

"Are you Mrs. Grace?" Nico asked.

Grace nodded. She pointed to Tiny's leash, which hung from a hook on the wall. Tiny trotted over, took the leash in his mouth and pulled it down. Then he sat waiting for his next command.

"And you are . . . ?" Grace asked.

"OOFOs, ma'am," Nico said.

"*Four* OOFOs! Jabo, Jabo, Jabo . . ." Grace sighed. "I don't suppose he told you we get ten first-of-Mays every week."

"Excuse me, ma'am," Nico said, "but it's not possible to have ten first-of-Mays."

Grace smiled. "It's what we call the new fellas. They show up beginning of tent season: the first day in May. Most of us would take a first-of-May over an OOFO any day."

"We're getting apprenticeships," Eugene explained.

Grace raised one eyebrow. "Jabo check that out with Diavolo?"

"Who is Diavolo?" Nico asked.

"He and Seraphina run the place. So did Jabo get his approval or not?"

Nico shrugged.

Grace shook her head. "Typical idea man—long on optimism, short on operations. I suppose an apprenticeship is possible, if you can walk on your hands while juggling with your feet?"

She searched their faces.

"Charm poisonous snakes? Walk a tightrope while balancing a chair on your nose?"

They shook their heads.

"Well, good luck to you, then." Grace gave a weak smile. "Wave goodbye, Tiny."

Tiny lifted one paw, then moved it back and forth. Grace moved her finger forward. Tiny jumped to his feet and leapt across the train car and down the stairwell to Grace. Grace snapped her fingers and he found his place next to her, still holding his leash in his mouth.

Even Doris smiled watching them. But as soon as they were gone, she said, "She thinks Jabo's a liar."

"No, she doesn't," Nico said.

"First he tried to scare us to death with that headless act, then he says we can get apprenticeships, when we can't," Doris said.

"Jabo's a good guy." Nico's voice was firm.

Doris rolled her eyes. "He's a good guy. Just like Frank," she said.

Lucy winced. Why did Doris always have to poke the part that hurt the most?

"We'll talk to him. He'll explain how it all works," Eugene said.

Lucy felt a surge of relief come over her. Eugene and Nico trusted Jabo, too.

Doris snorted, fingering a vase.

Eugene hovered over her. "Don't lose another chance," he said under his breath.

Doris glared at him, but she put the vase back and sat down to wait for Jabo, her two red noses in the curve of her lap.

* MONDAY, APRIL 17, 1939 *

....
CHAPTER TEN
....

"YOU USED TO TALK, LIKE EVERYBODY ELSE"

When they heard Jabo's footsteps approaching, Lucy and Eugene hustled out to help him carry a food hamper up the stairs.

"Sorry that took so long. Nitty-Bitty was in a mood. Had to pull out all the stops to procure this gastronomical sensation. Spaghetti, meatballs, and garlic bread: a tour de force, a taste heretofore unimaginable." Jabo wiped his hands with a polka-dotted hankie and began unloading salt and pepper shakers.

"Where's Tiny?" He searched their faces. "Ah, I see you've made the acquaintance of Lady Grace."

"She said we need to walk on our hands," Nico said.

"While juggling with our feet," Eugene added.

"Or charm snakes," Doris said.

79

Jabo nodded. "No doubt that would be helpful. Think big, my compatriots. Your life is just beginning. There is no telling what you're capable of. Now let's enjoy our supper while it's at optimal temperature for culinary appreciation. And then I will answer further queries as candidly as possible." He handed them each a rolled-up napkin.

Eugene and Lucy hovered around the basket as Jabo unloaded plates covered with checkered cloths. Lucy counted the plates as Jabo took them out. Five. They would each get their own!

She found a spot on the rug and sat cross-legged, breathing in the smell of tomatoes and garlic. On her plate were two big balls of meat! She stole a glance at the others. Did they all have such generous servings?

They did!

Jabo unrolled his napkin to reveal silverware. Lucy followed suit. Then she took a bite of the bread, which was toasted and warm, crunchy on the top and soft inside. She cut the round meat, the knife slipping through without sawing.

Lucy ate the meatballs fast, barely chewing. Anybody who got a good bite of meat at the orphanage knew to do this, or the bite would be swiped by a bigger girl. Lucy didn't think that would happen here, but the habit was hard to break.

The spaghetti was a challenge. Lucy had never eaten anything like it before. She watched to see how the others were managing. Doris dangled noodles one by one into her mouth. Eugene cut them into small pieces and scooped them with his spoon. Nico rolled the spaghetti around his fork and stuck the entire package into his mouth.

Jabo ate slowly with his fork upside down. Lucy rolled it the way Nico had, but spaghetti kept slipping off. She tried to stab the strands between the tines of her fork, but that didn't work, either. Finally, she rolled up a bigger bundle and managed to get that in her mouth.

"So," Jabo said, wiping his chin with his napkin, "you need to know what you're up against. The obstacles are substantial—some would say daunting."

Nico dabbed at his chin with his napkin, just as Jabo had. "What are the obstacles?" he asked.

"Usually we take OOFOs one at a time. It will be difficult to incorporate four new young people into our operation. And it is unlikely you'll get a performing apprenticeship, but there are behind-the-scenes positions within your reach."

Jabo cricked his neck and spoke in a quieter voice. "Though one of you will have a more challenging time acquiring an apprenticeship than the others."

Lucy, Nico, and Eugene turned to Bald Doris.

Doris stared back at them, her eyes hard as stale bread.

But Jabo was looking at her! Lucy's stomach began to churn.

"Lucy?" Nico whispered.

Jabo sighed. "I'm afraid so."

What had she done? He was turning on her like Mackinac had.

A big smile settled on Doris's lips.

Jabo's eyes traveled from Lucy and Nico seated on the floor to Eugene and Doris sharing the chair. "Danger is our stock-in-trade—our product, if you will. Every day any one of a thousand things can go perilously wrong. We depend on sharp young eyes to spot a loose harness, an unsecured cage, a cigarette smoldering in a straw bale. We need apprentices who can warn us this quick." He snapped his fingers. "There's no time to write a note. When you see trouble, you call 'John Robinson.' That means 'danger' in the circus business."

Lucy's nose felt like it had pepper inside. She made a fist, carving her nails into her palm. She would not cry.

"I'm sorry, Lucy," Jabo said.

Jabo was wrong. The words of her defense circled around her head, but there was no time to write them all down.

Lucy scribbled, *John Robinson.* Then she showed Jabo and sat back, waiting for his approving smile.

Jabo looked down at the paper, but his eyes did not light up. He continued on, his voice heavy. "You have to get someone's attention and be in close proximity to get them to read your paper, Lucy. A lot of circus people can't read English or they can't read at all. But every circus person knows 'John Robinson.'"

Jabo didn't understand. As long as Lucy kept her mouth shut, she was safe. Talking made her feel stupid—like she couldn't do anything right. Silence was how she protected herself.

"Here's what I suggest," Jabo said, addressing all of them. "Pay attention to what attracts you. I've given you a hint of my vision for you, but where you see yourself is of greater importance. Be polite and enthusiastic. There is always too much work to be done. Ready hands are your most powerful tools."

"How am I supposed to pay attention to two red rubber noses?" Bald Doris blurted out.

"That is a puzzle only you can solve, Mademoiselle Doris. Now, it's late and I have much to accomplish before tomorrow morning. I will procure your bedding. Then I'm afraid I must bid adieu.

"Eugene and Doris, can you provide assistance? Lucy, do you require more writing paper? There's a stack of old handbills in that corner, which you are welcome to utilize. The back side is blank."

Lucy nodded, her eyes on her shoes.

"Nico, would you care to try your hand at pencil sharpening?" Jabo handed a small blade and a brand-new pencil to Nico.

With Eugene, Doris, and Jabo gone, the train car grew quiet. Lucy listened to a horse whinnying in the distance, the scratch of Nico shaving the pencil, and the clicks and ticks of the clocks.

Lucy took the posters advertising the previous year's season and put a crease in the dancing horses so the white back would be ready to use.

Nico pushed the pencil shavings into a pile with the heel of his hand. "Hey," he whispered, not looking at her. "Did you know you talk in your sleep?"

Lucy gave him a sideways glance. She didn't know.

What do I say? she wrote.

"Mostly you mutter. But once you called out Milly or Billy."

Dilly. The dreams were so vivid, it hurt to have them. She could smell the spearmint gum Dilly liked to chew.

"Doris said you used to talk, like everybody else."

Lucy nodded stiffly.

Nico's finger touched the newly sharpened pencil point. "What happened?"

Lucy shoved the folded poster in her pocket. There was no way to explain how calm and in control she felt, so long as she didn't open her mouth. But the second the sounds came out, the criticism began. Miss Holland and Mackinac had drilled into her how embarrassing she was. Damaged. Ruined.

Writing had been the solution. It had made her feel that she could go on. She would not give it up.

"Lucy," Nico whispered. "Can you try? Here . . . with just me."

Lucy grabbed the pencil Nico had sharpened and took off.

"Lucy?" Nico's voice followed her down the stairs, but Lucy did not stop.

CHAPTER ELEVEN

AT THE BOTTOM OF THE SKINNY GRAY STICK OF A TAIL

It was cold and dark and Lucy hadn't stopped to grab her coat, but it felt good to leave the questions behind.

Even in her too-small shoes, running felt right. But where should she go?

Back to Bernadette's? Bernadette was an OOFO. Maybe she could convince her landlady to let one orphan stay in her boardinghouse. Bernadette would need help with her new baby.

But how would Lucy find her way back to Bernadette's? She didn't even know Bernadette's last name.

And Dilly . . . Lucy had thought Chicago was farther away from Riverport than it really was. Why hadn't Dilly tried to find her?

Lucy ran by little people soaking in an outside tub and a tall man in long underwear, ironing his trousers. She kept going until she could no longer see Jabo's train car.

Then she looked back at the flickering lights and breathed in the smell of hay, horse manure, sawdust, and something sweet—cinnamon, maybe.

Her belly was warm and full, but by tomorrow she'd be hungry. She couldn't just run away.

She'd find the elephant house. She'd prove herself there. She loved animals. Jabo had been right about that. When Jabo saw how valuable she was, he'd take back his words.

The map said the elephant house was on Water Street. If the streets made sense, Water Street would be by the river.

She thought she could hear the river and began walking toward it. She crossed a street with no street sign and the sound of the river grew louder.

When she got to the riverbank, she turned left but found only carpentry shops.

In the other direction, she spied a building that said CAMEL HOUSE.

The building next to the camel house had no sign. It had a row of square windows and an ordinary size door.

Lucy wanted to peek in the windows, but they were too high up.

Around the back of the building, she saw a small pond; a pile of chains; two big wooden chests; a stack of large, colorful tables; and two huge barn-size doors.

What was inside? Would she lose a chance for entering a barn without permission?

That was a risk she didn't want to take. She'd walk back to Jabo's home and ask him first.

But thinking about Jabo made her insides sting. She had thought he liked her best.

She stood chewing the inside of her cheek. She'd win him over again. Prove to him that a voice didn't matter.

She crept back around to the front of the building. Her hand slid over the door knob. The door swung open, and she tiptoed inside.

The barn was large and smelled of wet hay and laundry soap. Light radiated down from a loft.

In the back a bare lightbulb shone on a massive hunkered-down shape. It had four huge legs, a big head with flapping ears, and a strange ringed hose of a nose.

The elephant was at least twice the size of a large horse. Its legs were wider around than Lucy's waist. A metal chain anchored one giant flat foot to the floor.

But it was the trunk that fascinated her. It curved around a carrot and then shoved it into the wet pink triangle of its mouth. The chewing sound was deep and amplified.

The elephant had big flat wrinkly cheeks and small eyes with dark pupils and long eyelashes, which made Lucy think the animal was a girl. Lucy longed to touch her great flapping ears and that strange ridged trunk that ended in a delicate curl. She felt comfortable with this great beast.

The elephant continued to put leaves, vegetables, and hay into her mouth. When she got too many carrots, she parked one between the short white tusks on either side of her head until her mouth was ready for that one, too. She ate fast and furiously, like an orphanage girl.

On the elephant's back, wiry black hairs sprang from thick hide. Lucy took the elephant hairs from her pocket. This elephant's hairs were similar to the hairs Jabo had given her, but curly, not straight.

Lucy moved around the elephant until she could see her tail. It was too small for the enormous backside, as if it belonged to another animal entirely. At the bottom of the skinny gray stick of a tail was a brush of wiry hair.

Lucy moved toward her. The elephant turned her head, her small eyes taking in her visitor. Lucy reached out and the wet tip of the elephant's trunk touched her arm! She moved closer and patted the elephant's wrinkled chest. It felt like living leather.

The elephant encircled another carrot with her trunk and stuffed it in her mouth, crunching loudly. Then Lucy heard someone call her name. She jumped.

But it was only Nico.

"Get out of there," he whispered.

Lucy shook her head, then turned back to the elephant. She was going to be an elephant girl. He would see. They all would.

"Lucy," Nico warned.

Lucy could hear Nico breathing behind her, but she held her ground.

"You see anyone? We don't want to lose a chance," Nico whispered.

Lucy shook her head.

"Let's go," Nico said.

Nico was right, but it felt impossible to leave.

Lucy ran her fingers over the elephant's trunk. Then she followed Nico out. They stayed in the shadow of the wall, their eyes on the square of light glowing from the loft. Someone lived up there.

Lucy's fingers tingled with the feel of the elephant's thick, wrinkled hide. She would find a way to get the elephant trainer to take her on she decided as they ran down to the river's edge, the moon shining on the water in a glistening line.

Nico was watching her. He seemed to almost know what she was thinking, because he said, "You're lucky. You know what you want. I got mustaches." He shook his head. "Am I supposed to be a barber?"

Lucy laughed.

Nico smiled. "Look," he said. "I'm sorry, okay? I didn't mean to put you on the spot like that. . . . If you want to leave, I'll go with you."

A warm feeling came over her. Nico was her friend.

"Do you want to go back to Chicago? I mean . . ."

Nico faced her squarely. "Didn't you say your sister lives there?"

Lucy nodded.

"I've been thinking. We got Frank and Alice at a bad time is all."

They started walking back.

"Frank taught me a lot. He'll have to start all over with Willy," Nico said.

Lucy tried to make sense of this. Hadn't Nico said he'd been at the orphanage for one hundred and ninety-something days? Six months. Enough time for Frank and Alice to have worked things out with Willy.

"Willy's too young to understand money," Nico said.

Lucy chewed her lip. Money wasn't that complicated, and Willy wasn't that young.

"You got to figure out how it works. Who has money. Who owes money. Then you know who has the power and why."

She frowned at him.

"It's like the kitchen-chore kids."

At the orphanage, you had to know who to go to for things. Who to stay away from. Who to let in front of you in line, because if you didn't your bed would be wet every night when you climbed in.

The kitchen-chore kids were useful, because they could steal food. Lucy had received a slice of bread in exchange for helping one of them study for a test once.

"Soon as Frank and Alice and I got to a new place, we'd

have to figure all that out. They need me. I doubt Willy could tell a good card hand from a bad one."

Lucy's face registered her question.

Nico nodded. He was good at reading her expressions.

"Frank plays poker. He'd say, 'Nico, my cigarettes.' If I handed them to him with my left hand, it meant his cards weren't as strong as the other man's. But it was tricky. You had to look at the other guy's cards without him seeing you. That's why being young and small for my age helped. People don't suspect little kids."

Eugene had mentioned this.

"Frank doesn't like to have things sprung on him. Just showing up, all four of us like that. I should have known better."

He was talking fast, like the orphanage girls waiting for their mamas on visiting day. Every week they waited. But their mamas didn't come.

Frank and Alice had walked away. Bernadette had helped them, and she was a complete stranger.

The wind lifted Lucy's hair off her neck and played with the hem of her dress. But the wind didn't change the dark river's path. The water kept going in one direction, splitting around the rocks in its way. The river didn't go backward. It always went forward.

"Don't you want to find your sister?" Nico asked.

She nodded, thinking about the look on Frank's face when Doris touched his coat. Frank wouldn't help Lucy find Dilly. He wouldn't help any of them.

If they all got apprenticeships, they would go with the circus to Chicago. Then Lucy would find Dilly.

But Dilly was the most persistent person Lucy knew. She would have written Lucy if she wanted to. Maybe Dilly didn't want to be found.

January 17, 1939
Home for Friendless Children
Riverport, Iowa

Dear Mrs. Mackinac,

Thank you for sending the photograph. That is not my Lucy. My sister has red curly hair & freckles. She is small for her age. When I saw her last, she was the height of a sewing machine, the weight of a sack of flour.

She likes to sing songs she makes up in her head. She is a good reader and fast with her sums.

I have enough $$ for her train ticket home. Please could you gather all your girls together and call out Lucy Sauvé and she will raise her hand. Then ask her the name of the bachelor downstairs. When I see his name in your letter, I will mail you $$ for her ticket. If you could, please send her with a basket of supper so she won't get hungry on the train.

Yours truly,
Dilly Sauvé

January 18, 1939

Dear Lucy,

I guess some other Lucy will be reading the letter I wrote to you all about our private business or else it got throwed away.

I am not sending this letter until I know for sure where you are at. But it felt good all up inside myself to write to you last time, so I'm writing again. I will keep this letter in my top dresser drawer with the letter Mama wrote to me.

I set up a corner of my room for you. On the walls I pinned pictures of hats from a magazine, because I don't draw them as well as Mama did. I have a bag of peanuts because you love them so. Mama and I would laugh about how we would know you were in a room by the peanut smell.

I have three books in your corner. I got them from a correspondence course to make myself improved. It did not take. I'm still regular old me. I would rather sew dresses than read, because when I'm done sewing I have a new dress and when I'm done reading I have stories in my head that make me wonder about the world. It's okay to wonder, but not when you have nobody to talk to about the wondering.

It's late now & I have to be up early so no one else

will get my sewing machine, #71. It is the best machine in all of Mrs. LaFinestre's sewing shop & I take extra careful care of it the way Mama did with her one pair of high-heel shoes, remember?

Love,
Dilly

CHAPTER TWELVE

"EVER SINCE MACKINAC PICKED HER"

When they got back to Jabo's, Lucy was happy to see Jabo wasn't there. She didn't want to have to explain to him where they'd been.

Eugene and Doris were sitting up talking in beds they'd made on the floor.

"We got extra cookies," Doris gloated. "And you lost a chance."

Lucy's insides turned to sludge.

"Why?" Nico asked.

"Not supposed to go snooping around without asking. Someone told Diavolo," Doris crowed.

They'd lost a chance and it was Lucy's fault. How had she let this happen?

I'm sorry, Lucy wrote, handing the page to Nico.

Eugene worked a package out of his pocket and unwrapped the wax paper. Inside was a small stack of peanut butter cookies. He offered them to Nico and Lucy.

"Don't give those away," Doris hissed at Eugene. "That's why Mama didn't want you. She said you weren't smart enough to figure out how the world works."

The spark in Eugene's eyes went out. He gave an unconvincing shrug. "She sent you away too," he whispered.

"She couldn't help that," Doris said.

Lucy and Nico stared at Doris.

"Why are you so mean?" Nico asked.

"Well, it's true."

"You don't tell the whole truth. Only the mean part," Nico said.

"I don't know what you're talking about," Doris said.

Nico took a bite of his cookie. "Yes, you do."

Lucy popped a piece in her mouth and the sweet, nutty brown sugar melted on her tongue. The taste reminded her of eating peanuts on the fire escape with Dilly.

Nico eyed Doris. "We got to have each other's backs."

"You left, not me," Doris said.

Doris was like the skin burn you got when someone twisted your arm in two directions. It pained you to agree with her, even when she was right.

Nico's head nodded one-eighth of an inch. "From now on . . . all of us or none of us." His eyes found Lucy's. She nodded and he offered his hand to Doris, who shook it.

Then they all took turns shaking each other's hands.

"We should talk about tomorrow," Nico said. "Lucy's going to try for elephant girl. What about you two?"

"Fortune-teller," Doris said.

"A working guy that puts up the tents," Eugene said. "Roustabouts, they're called. What about you?"

"Gonna try to get closer to Jabo," Nico said. "We need to know how this place works."

This was smart. The more they knew about Saachi's, the better.

Two small pillows and two stacks of blankets sat on the floor next to Eugene. *Lucy* read an elegantly printed note pinned to the top of one stack. *Nico* read the note fixed to the other.

Jabo made sure they were taken care of. He seemed considerate of everyone. Lucy just needed to explain to him why she couldn't talk. Then he would understand.

Lucy made her bed on the floor between Eugene and Nico. Then, when everyone was asleep, she got out her paper and pencil and began to write.

Dear Jabo,
    I understand how important it is to be able to say "John Robinson." I know this is why I need to talk. But some things are a permanent part of a person, like how the Chicken Man always wears his chicken suit, and the Zebra Lady can't take off her stripes.

My quiet is a part of me. It is as important to me as being ringmaster is to you.

I'll be the best apprentice Saachi's Circus Spectacular has ever had. I'll teach "John Robinson" hand signals to every person. There will never be a danger that I see that everyone in the circus won't know about.

Please don't make me speak.

Sincerely,

Lucy Simone Sauvé

Lucy set the letter on Jabo's pillow. Then she lay down in her spot, tucking the blankets under her chin.

She felt good about what she had written, but bad about losing her chance and Nico's. Mostly, though, her mind was spinning with thoughts about the elephant.

Lucy would feed the elephant. She would water the elephant. Did you brush an elephant? Did you comb its tail?

The elephant liked her already, Lucy was sure of it.

Her head sank deeper into the pillow.

The next thing Lucy knew the room was shrinking and the lady from the university, Miss Holland, was shouting, her long white fingers were strangling Lucy.

"Every time you open your mouth, you embarrass yourself and humiliate Mrs. Mackinac."

"Lucy! Lucy!" Jabo shook her gently. "It's just a bad dream. You're safe here with us."

Lucy opened her eyes.

It was dark in Jabo's train car. Jabo in his striped robe was on one side of her, Doris in her orphanage dress on the other.

"You had a nightmare. That's all." Jabo patted her back. "You're with us now. Everything is going to be fine."

Lucy nodded. Cold sweat ran down her sides.

"She has a lot of nightmares. Ever since Mackinac picked her," Doris reported.

Jabo's eyes turned a deeper brown. "Do you want to talk about your dream?" he whispered, handing Lucy a pencil and paper.

Lucy shook her head.

Miss Holland made her feel like dirt. Lucy tried so hard with her, but she couldn't get her mouth to say the words the way Miss Holland wanted. Couldn't speak without pausing, stuttering.

Jabo stroked her hair gently, like Mama would when she had a fever. "You're safe now. Remember, you're an OOFO. And OOFOs are protected by the great order of orphans everywhere. We look out for each other."

Lucy nodded.

"Try to get some sleep. We've got a big day tomorrow." His joints cracked as he stood up. He hopped onto the step by his bed, and climbed in, folding the covers over his shoulders.

Eugene snored softly, still holding his cards in his hand. Nico breathed in fits and starts, one mustache stuck crookedly across his lip. The clocks tick-tocked and tick-tick-ticked, for what seemed like a long time before she heard Jabo's gentle sleep-breathing. Doris was still sitting up, her eyes open. At the orphanage, she was the one awake when you went to the bathroom in the middle of the night.

"Sing, please," she whispered to Lucy.

The first few years in the orphanage, Lucy had sung to the little girls every night. All the girls looked forward to hearing her. They would pretend to be asleep until the night matron got up from the chair, closed the door of the girls' dorm room, and walked down the hall. Then Lucy would begin to sing.

"Please, Lucy," Doris begged. "You know you can."

Lucy picked up her blankets and moved them next to Doris. When she was settled, she reached her hand out and Doris took it. A few minutes later Doris too was asleep.

CHAPTER THIRTEEN

"THE ONE YOU GOT TO WORRY ABOUT"

The next thing Lucy knew, Jabo was announcing, "Rise and shine. Cook tent flag's up."

It was still dark out, but the lights in the old train car were on. Nico was using his fingers to comb his hair. Eugene and Doris waited by the door with freshly washed faces. Lucy folded her blankets and went to the tiny bathroom to clean up.

"We get to go to the cook tent," Doris announced when Lucy came out.

"Yes. I spoke with Diavolo and Seraphina last night," Jabo explained. "They agreed to give you six days to secure an apprenticeship."

"Six days?" Nico asked.

Jabo cracked his knuckles. "Yes, Saturday is dress rehearsal and then we boil up. First performance is Sunday here in Karaboo. We leave when we're done with the show."

"Boil up?" Nico asked as Jabo rifled through the tools and broken timepieces on his workbench.

"In a manner of speaking, my fine sir. Means we take baths. Boil clothes." Jabo slipped a pocket watch into his vest. "Ready?" he asked.

They followed him down the stairs and across the muddy ground by the horse corrals. The dark outside was beginning to loosen its grip. The first sliver of orange cut through the gray.

When they got to the entrance of the cook tent, Jabo gathered them in a huddle. "Listen up, OOFOs. Two sides to the cook tent. Performers on the right, working people on the left. You'll sit with the working people: the candy butchers, canvas men, roustabouts, menagerie. Listen to them. They know who is light-handed, who will be likely to take an apprentice on, and who to look out for."

"Do I have to be a clown?" Doris burst out.

"Of course not, Mademoiselle Doris. You'll find your own true star in our spinning galaxy," Jabo said as he moved through the flap door into the cook tent.

Inside, a checked curtain hung on a rope between the sides. On the right side were tall people, short people, dark skinned, light skinned, illustrated, and zebra striped . . . everyone was talking and laughing.

Lucy saw a man so tall that even sitting down, he towered over the waiter. A table full of dwarfs. A woman with a mustache.

On the left side there were a few women and lots of big, burly men.

A pass-through window at the front of the tent had steaming dishes of potatoes, bacon, sausage, and stacks of pancakes. Beyond the window was the kitchen, full of sparkling appliances, pots and pans, and stacks of dishes. The cook tent kitchen could not have been more different from the worn walls and floors and iron pots of the orphanage kitchen.

"Don't stare, and remember, make yourself useful," Jabo whispered to Doris as a slight lady with a white cook's hat appeared behind them. The cook had a wrinkled face and lively dark eyes.

"Best to put them at different tables," the cook said.

Jabo bowed to her. "You are as gracious as you are lovely, Nitty-Bitty."

"I'm nothing of the kind, you rascal," Nitty-Bitty growled, shaking her finger at him. "Don't you sugar-talk me." But the corner of Nitty-Bitty's mouth twitched as she fought back a smile.

Jabo laughed. "Nitty's right. It's best you split up."

Doris clamped her hand around Eugene's. Lucy and Nico exchanged a look. All of them wanted to sit together.

A dwarf in a polka-dotted dress walked by. Her hair was pasted flat against her head with a wave at the bottom. An unlit cigarette hung between bright pink lips. "Don't tell me. Jabo's back to OOFOing," she muttered in a raspy voice as she walked by.

"Dame Catherine is one of our biggest stars." Jabo nodded to her. "Lucy, the table in the back there. Nico, the one here. Doris and Eugene, you come with me."

Lucy's knees wobbled as she headed for her table. Three extra-large men were hunkered over their plates. She breathed in the smell of sweat, tobacco, maple syrup, and sausages.

She sat down on the bench and a waiter in kitchen whites placed a plate piled high with pancakes and sausages in front of her. A little squeal of pleasure escaped her mouth.

The men laughed and Lucy's cheeks turned hot.

She had just tucked into her pancakes when the man closest to her, with hands big and lumpy as potatoes, said, "Hello."

Lucy waved her fork at him.

"Name's Bunk. That's Rib with the big ears. Nevada." He pointed to a man with wavy hair. "Watch out for him or he'll eat the food right off your plate. You're an OOFO, that right?"

Lucy nodded.

"What's your name?" Bunk asked.

Lucy put down her fork, found the part of her paper where she had written *Lucy,* and showed Bunk.

Rib knit his brow.

"An OOFO that don't say nothing. That's something," Nevada said.

"Be a blessing you kept your mouth shut," Bunk said.

They all laughed.

Lucy gobbled down her sausage.

"Hold on to your plates, boys. The girl's got an appetite," Rib said.

"Eats like a roustabout," Bunk said. "Make a muscle." He flexed his arm to demonstrate.

Lucy bent her arm and closed her fist.

Bunk felt her biceps, then shook his head. "I don't think so."

Rib patted the top of her head. "Hair's sure red, and it got springs. Surely that's useful for something."

Lucy picked up her pencil and wrote *Elephants*.

Bunk nodded. "Grace could use an extra set of hands, I expect, but . . ." His voice trailed off.

The hot cakes went cold in Lucy's mouth. She picked up her pencil and began to write fast and furious.

"Sparks coming off that pencil." Rib winked at Bunk.

Jabo gave me three elephant hairs.

She handed the page to Rib, who passed it to Bunk.

"Jabo." Bunk nodded. "Everybody loves that man, Nitty-Bitty, Lady Grace, Betts—they're good people. The one you got to worry about is—"

"Diavolo," Nevada whispered.

"Yup. And we work for him," Rib said under his breath.

"I'll point him out, but don't say anything," Bunk warned.

"Guess you don't got to worry none about that." Rib grinned.

Bunk laughed. "Come on. We'll act like we're helping the

waiters out." He dumped the rest of the sausages on Nevada's plate, then carried the serving dish up to the front.

Diavolo was seated at the front table on the performers' side, his feet perched on a velvet footstool. He was a slight man with shiny black hair and a thin mustache that reminded Lucy of Nico's mustache gifts. He rang a bell and Nitty-Bitty came running.

"He's superstitious. Got to have his plate just so," Bunk whispered, exchanging the empty sausage plate for a full one. "Temperamental, too. The man's got a thirst for danger. Lives for it. And he's got to win. Even if it's something little like guessing the number of jelly beans in a jar."

Lucy nodded.

"And that's his wife, Seraphina," Bunk said. "We all love her."

A woman with long hair, black and shiny as tar, sat next to him. She had dark eyes and muscular arms.

"Stay away from Diavolo," Nevada said when they got back to the roustabout table.

"Be careful of that guy, too." Rib poked Bunk.

Bunk laughed. "Finish up and I'll take you to meet Grace. I'll put in a good word for you."

"A good word from Bunk means a lot," Rib whispered to Lucy.

Bunk pulled out a piece of newspaper and handed it to her. He pointed to the serving platter. "Wrap the sausages and put 'em in your pocket."

"You can starve to death between meals," Rib agreed.

"But stay away from the big cats. They are fond of sausages," Nevada said.

"Stay away from them anyway. What else can we tell her might help her out, boys?" Bunk asked as Lucy rolled the sausages in the paper and stuck them in her pocket.

"You watch Grace with her animals and think you can do what she can, you got another think coming," Nevada said.

"She does the strong-woman act, then Elephantoff. Plus, the menagerie men report to her. Makes it all look easy."

"But she don't suffer fools," Rib said.

"Must be why she doesn't talk to you, Rib," Bunk said.

Again, they laughed.

"Seriously, Lucy, Saachi's is its own kind of special," Bunk said. "A home for those of us don't fit in anywhere else."

Lucy smiled.

"What do you think, boys. Is she a keeper?"

"You bet," Rib said.

Nevada nodded. "Gotta make sure Grace takes her on."

"I'll do my best." Bunk stood up. "Come on. Let's go see Grace."

CHAPTER FOURTEEN

"OUR NEW FAVORITE OOFO"

Lucy half skipped, half ran to the elephant barn with Bunk. When they arrived, morning light was streaming in the open back doors and the air smelled of hay and rotten fruit. The elephant was standing in the same place as the night before, but there was a second elephant, a much smaller one with the same wrinkly, saggy gray skin and huge flapping ears.

The baby elephant was playing with an empty basket. Turning it upside down. Setting it right-side up. Taking a trunk full of sawdust and sprinkling it on her back. The baby's trunk was as useful as an arm with a hand attached.

"The little elephant is Baby. She's a year old. The large one is Jenny. She's not Baby's mama, but she doesn't seem to know that," Bunk explained.

Lucy wanted to touch the elephants, but she didn't dare with Bunk standing next to her and Grace in the feed room.

Bunk took off his hat and waited. Grace had a long-legged walk that made her seem to glide through space.

Grace smiled at Bunk like he was the only person in the universe she wanted to see. "You again? How am I supposed to get my work done with you visiting all the time?"

"Better figure it out. Otherwise, I'll have to." Bunk winked at Lucy.

"Do my work? That I'd like to see," Grace said.

"Me too." Bunk grinned.

Grace looked over at Lucy. "And you are . . . ?"

"Lucy, meet Grace. She's our new favorite OOFO, and she's got her heart set on being a bull girl," Bunk said.

A bull girl? Lucy shook her head. She wanted to work with the elephants.

"That's what we call elephants around here," Bunk whispered.

Grace raised one eyebrow.

"She's a little green," Bunk said, "but we got a good feeling about her."

Grace snorted. "I can't help but notice you're not taking her on."

"Don't think she's cut out for tenting work," Bunk said.

Grace nodded. "I'll give her a try provided you stay with Baby during the performance."

"Rib okay?" Bunk asked.

"What about the word *you* wasn't clear?"

"Yes, ma'am, it will be me." Bunk nodded. "Go get 'em," he whispered to Lucy, and hurried out.

Grace walked out the back door. Lucy followed, taking stock of the small pond, the stack of hay bales that towered over her, and the brightly painted round, low tables. Grace pointed to the tables, handing her a bucket and a sponge. "Those stands need washing."

The stands were covered with a thick coat of dust, but they cleaned up nicely. While Lucy worked, she wondered what exactly Grace had meant by "give her a try"? Was the apprenticeship hers, so long as she did a good job?

Lucy had washed two stands when Grace reappeared. "Jabo gave me an earful about how I need to give you OOFOs a chance," she said, and sighed. "What makes you think you can handle an elephant?"

Lucy reached into her pocket. But her dress was wet and so was the paper.

"Speak up, girl. I don't have all day," Grace barked.

Lucy opened her mouth to answer. But all she could hear was Miss Holland. *"People judge you by the way you speak. Nobody wants to be around someone like you stumbling over every word. You will always be alone."*

Lucy clamped her teeth together and began scrubbing the third stand. Mama used to say if you're a hard worker, there will always be a job for you.

Grace stood watching, towering over Lucy. Her voice was gentler now. "Lucy?"

Lucy turned.

"Do you speak English?" she asked.

Lucy nodded.

"But you don't talk?"

Lucy shook her head.

Grace groaned. "Great balls of fire, Jabo."

Lucy began writing as fast as she could on her wet paper. This was her chance. She had to convince Grace, but before she could finish, a familiar voice called out, "We work together, ma'am."

Doris! Where had she come from?

Grace looked Doris up and down. "You want to be a bull girl too, I take it?"

"Yes, ma'am." Doris curtseyed. "I'm Doris."

Grace angled her head toward Lucy. "She's mute?"

"She used to talk, but not anymore. She can still sing, though, *when she wants to,*" Doris said.

"Oh, for Pete's sake," Grace muttered, fishing work gloves out of her pocket and slipping them on. "Why'd she stop talking?"

"She got mad," Doris said.

"Mad?"

Doris nodded. "Matron Mackinac liked her a real lot. She was always saying, 'Girls, Lucy didn't miss one single spelling

word. Girls, you would do well to follow Lucy's example,'"
Doris sniped, imitating Mackinac. "Then Lucy started to
have these lessons with a lady from the university. After that,
Mackinac only had mean things to say about her, and Lucy
stopped talking."

Lucy's face got hot. She stared at Doris. It was unnerving
to hear what happened from her point of view.

"What kind of lessons?" Grace asked.

"We thought they were singing lessons, but—" Doris shook
her head.

Grace's face tightened. "I have seventeen animals and six
menagerie workers. I can't have a bull girl that doesn't speak."

"Everybody always wants Lucy on their chore crew. She
does more than her share. I got a voice you can hear a mile
away. We're a good team, ma'am," Doris said.

Grace gave Doris an appraising look.

"Did everybody want you on their chore crew, Doris?"

"Oh yes, ma'am," Doris said.

Grace wiped her ear with her shoulder. "Doris, you got
the morning to prove yourself. I'm only giving you this chance
because I owe Jabo. Lucy, I can't have you around my animals.
It isn't safe. Do you understand?"

Give me a chance. You won't be disappointed, Lucy wrote.

By the time she'd finished, Grace had disappeared. Lucy
found her in the feed room packing ropes, brushes, and lini-
ment into a wooden crate.

Lucy thrust the page at her.

Grace didn't take it. "I made my decision, Lucy," she snapped.

Lucy walked toward the elephants. They were all she'd thought about since last night.

Why did it matter that she didn't talk?

She was a good listener. And by writing her answers, she was forced to think harder about what she wanted to say.

Lucy tried to get Jenny's attention, but she was busy eating. Baby moved her trunk toward Lucy.

"Lucy, did you hear what I said?" Grace glared at her.

Lucy slunk out of the elephant barn. How come Bald Doris got to work with the elephants? Doris got clown noses, not elephant hairs.

Lucy wanted to be mad at Doris. But Doris had tried to get Grace to take them both on. Working as a team had been a good idea.

On her own, Bald Doris wouldn't last a week with Grace. But they were leaving on Sunday. Doris might last until then.

Lucy would need to find another apprenticeship.

The sewing shop, maybe.

Mama had taught her to hem and baste. She wasn't a seamstress, but maybe she could be an apprentice.

When you were sewing you were supposed to keep your mouth shut and do your work. That's what Mama had said. There was no real danger in a sewing shop. No reason to have to shout "John Robinson."

The costume shop was on the other side of Winter Quarters. She headed past the prop shop, past the cook tent, where a waiter was wiping down empty tables, past the fortune-telling booth with its shimmering curtains.

The costume shop had bolts of fabric, a dressmaker's bust, and three sewing machines. Standing on a pedestal by a large mirror, Diavolo stood peering at himself. He was wearing a white shirt, a red silk vest, and gray trousers.

A pregnant lady in a yellow polka-dotted dress watched him, measuring tape in hand.

"It inhibits the motion of my left arm! How many stitches did you use?" Diavolo barked.

"Forty-five, same as the right," the seamstress said.

"You are not careful."

"I'm very careful," she said.

Lucy backed away. She didn't want anything to do with Diavolo. But he caught sight of her in the mirror. "Diavolo doesn't know you," he announced.

"Can I help you?" the seamstress asked.

Lucy took out the soggy page and wrote as best she could. But before she could hand her paper to the seamstress, Diavolo snatched it out of her hands and read out loud, " 'I'm Lucy. I'm an OOFO and I can sew a little.' "

"Hello, Lucy." The seamstress smiled warmly. "I'm Betts, and this is Diavolo."

"What's the matter with you?" Diavolo demanded.

Lucy's head dipped to write her answer.

115

"'Don't talk. Listen very well,'" Diavolo read, a smile blooming on his lips. He bowed and made a grand gesture offering Lucy his hand. "Pleased to meet you, Lucy."

Lucy smiled. She wasn't expecting this.

"How tall are you?" he murmured, leaping gracefully off the alterations pedestal. He moved as if every step was a dance. "A little over four feet, I'd say," he answered for her.

"Nooooo," Betts whispered.

"She's an OOFO. She has to find an apprenticeship," Diavolo said.

"She wants to work for me," Betts said, "don't you?"

Lucy nodded.

"You need a real seamstress, not an apprentice. She's Diavolo's," he said.

Betts crossed her arms, resting them on her big belly. She glared at him.

"Need I remind you how important it is for us to make money this season?" Diavolo asked.

"What's that got to do with anything?"

"Danger, Betts. Danger is what they come for. You know that as well as I do. Wait here, Lucy." He disappeared behind a curtain.

Lucy took out her paper and wrote *Danger?* but before she could show Betts, Diavolo swept out of the dressing room wearing a leotard and tight-fitting pants. He handed the white shirt and the red silk vest to Betts. "I need these by noon."

Then he bowed to Lucy. "Lucy, my sweet girl, you have

yourself an apprenticeship with the great, the one and only Diavolo. I'll let Jabo know. Now let's go."

Betts stared at Lucy, a hollow look in her eyes.

This was only temporary, Lucy told herself. Just until she could convince Grace to take her on.

CHAPTER FIFTEEN

BREATHING LESSONS

Diavolo was a short, slender man, but he walked in big angry strides, his hand firmly wrapped around Lucy's. She had to run to keep up.

A roustabout jumped out of their way, tipping his hat to Diavolo. A juggler caught his pins and bowed. The acrobats tracked Diavolo's progress under hooded lids as they rubbed white chalk on their hands.

Lucy tried to calm herself, but a thousand questions chased around her head. Did he know she wasn't an acrobat? Did he know she'd never been on a high wire? Did he know she couldn't walk on her hands while juggling with her feet?

Still, it was good to have powerful people on your side. That was why Nico wanted to work for Jabo, and Diavolo was Jabo's boss.

The cook tent flag was down, but when Nitty-Bitty saw Diavolo, she dashed out with a quart bottle of cold water.

"Half-filled with ice?" Diavolo asked.

"Yes, sir." Nitty-Bitty nodded, her voice stiff, nothing like the raspy, teasing way she spoke to Jabo.

Diavolo led Lucy behind the big top to a large tent. Outside the tent stood two large men with shoulders that nearly busted out of their shirts and necks bigger around than a lady's waist.

"Diavolo doesn't need anything this morning. Report to Bunk," Diavolo told them as he led Lucy inside the tent, which had mirrors all around and sparkly costumes hanging from a bar. Diavolo flipped through the clothes, considering shimmery gold pants before settling on a sparkly burgundy dress. He eyeballed her feet, then dug through a basket of shoes and handed her a pair of black flats.

"Give yourself a sponge bath and comb that hair. Put on your costume. In the dressing room." He nodded to a piece of canvas stretched along a rope on one side of the tent.

"Quickly, please." He handed her a bucket of water. "Diavolo does not like to wait."

On the other side of the canvas curtain, Lucy yanked off her shoes and slipped on the new ones. Even with the blisters and her purple-bruised toes, the new shoes felt good.

The water in the bucket was cold. She shivered as she wiped the dirt and grime off her arms and face.

"Don't make Diavolo wait!" Diavolo barked on the other side of the curtain.

Lucy slipped on the dress, which was thick with sequins, sparkles, and dangling jewels. She tied the belt twice around her waist to make it fit, but she could do nothing about the straps that slid off her arms. She blushed. A young lady should not be seen in a dress like this.

In the mirror she was shocked to see her sunken cheeks and the dark gray under her eyes. There were no mirrors at the orphanage. The girls caught their reflections in the window of the dining hall at night.

Her hair needed combing, but that was nothing new. Her kind of hair needed combing the minute she stopped combing it.

The dress had no pockets, so she left the vocabulary words and her baby tooth in the pocket of the orphanage dress. She shoved her pencil and paper in her drawers and tucked Dilly's button and the silk purse with the elephant hair under the arch of her foot. She would have liked to keep the button in her hand, but she didn't think she could swing from a bar and hold on to it at the same time. Even with her stuff inside, these shoes were like walking on soft grass. She felt grateful for every step.

When she came out, Diavolo shook his head. "All wrong for you, but I like the idea of a child. So vulnerable." His fingers stroked his chin. "A pinafore, maybe, with a big bow and a lollipop. I'll get Betts working on it." He smiled.

"The last girl was a screamer. Gave me migraines. A mute is brilliant."

Lucy smiled. Finally someone who appreciated this part of her!

"Now let's get to work. Stand up straight and hold still." He walked around her, nodding. "What is this?" He patted the hip where her pencil and paper were hidden.

Lucy's cheeks flushed.

"Get rid of it."

She ducked behind the curtain, pulled out her pencil and paper, and set them with her orphanage dress. She pushed the silk purse deeper into her shoes and came back out.

"Stand still." Diavolo's nostrils flared. "You're holding your breath. Breathe evenly. *E-ven-ly.* Each breath the same. The tick of a clock is not one long, one short. Each tick. Is. The. Same."

Why did it matter how she breathed?

Lucy sucked in air with her mouth open and then closed. Diavolo pounded a tambourine, commanding her to breathe to its rhythm.

"Say the alphabet. Count in your head. Breathe to the letter. Breathe to the count." Diavolo had so many suggestions and he made her try every one. He acted as if she'd never taken a single breath in her entire life and it was his job to teach her how.

Lucy focused on the numbers. She breathed to the count.

"Too fast," he shouted.

He had her close her eyes. Place her fingers on her chest. Do short hops breathing in rhythm. She breathed in with one number, out with the other. She opened her nostrils and tried to breathe like a machine.

They spent most of the morning with Diavolo pounding the tambourine, until finally he nodded. "That'll do. Now, that hair." He moved to his dressing table, uncorked a small bottle, and shook drops onto Lucy's hand.

"Smooth it down. No stray hairs. None!"

Lucy went to work slathering greasy pomade on her head, but it was tough to tame the thick corkscrew strands. Would he yell at her for using too much? Not enough?

When she was done, Diavolo shook his head and poured more drops on her hand. Lucy went through her hair again, until it was shiny with grease and slicked back like she'd just gotten out of a bath.

He picked up another glass bottle marked GINGER. "Do you get motion sick?"

Lucy shook her head.

He smiled at her. "I'm liking you more and more all the time."

He dabbed oil on her wrists. This one smelled like oranges. "Put a little under your nose. Scent is calming," he said.

Calming?

"Okay. We're ready to go. We'll start slowly. I like a long warm-up."

Why hadn't Diavolo tested to see how strong she was? Or asked if she was afraid of heights? Wouldn't you want to know this about an acrobat apprentice?

They stopped by a small stage with ropes hanging from a wooden platform three stories high. A man in a leotard swooped through the air on a high trapeze.

Lucy's stomach twisted.

The aerialist swung from bar to rope to bar while Diavolo fussed around her. He had her stand with her back against a large, flat plywood circle. He adjusted the risers so she could reach the handles on either side and buckled straps over her ankles.

"Ready?" he asked.

She nodded uncertainly.

"I'm going to make it spin."

He hadn't believed her when she said she didn't get motion sick. This was a test.

Diavolo fiddled with the mechanism behind the plywood circle.

The air smelled of pomade and sweat. On the other side of the tent, a woman balanced another woman on her head. How was that even possible? A man dressed in purple pants stood on a ladder, juggling rings; a woman sat reading a book with her legs bent in a way it wasn't possible for legs to bend. Her toes turned the pages.

Lucy's limbs went stiff.

"Ready? Stay still, count, and breathe." Diavolo cranked the lever of a motor behind the plywood circle. The motor caught with a *ch-tick-ch-tick-ch-tick,* then began to whir. Lucy started to spin.

Everything went upside down. Right-side up. Upside down. The whirring grew louder; the machine spun faster. The world was a streaming swoosh round and round.

"Good," Diavolo shouted as the wheel began to slow. And the whoosh of color became the sky and the ground and the shapes of recognizable things. Upside down, right-side up. Then back and forth, until finally the wheel came to a stop.

"Not bad," Diavolo said.

Lucy's head felt woozy, but she smiled at Diavolo. She liked how encouraging he was. Maybe Bunk and Rib had been wrong about him. He could be difficult, but he could also be nice.

"All right." He nodded.

She waited for him to unstrap her legs. She was looking forward to stepping off the wheel and standing on solid ground.

"Okay, then. Keep counting and breathing, like we practiced. Don't decide to scratch your head or shoo a fly or wipe your nose. Do you understand?" He stared hard at her with his riveting eyes.

Lucy gave a small nod. Hadn't she already passed the test?

"We won't make it spin. Not yet," he called to her.

That was good. She breathed a sigh of relief.

A minute later, she heard metal clanking. She didn't move her head to look. She would show Diavolo that she could follow instructions.

A flurry of motion. Out of the corner of her eye, something shiny: blades lodged in a table, handle sides up.

Knives!

Diavolo had one in each hand. He was tossing them into the air and catching them by their handles.

He was going to throw knives at her!

The blood drained out of her head. Sweat dripped down her back. Her heart flung itself against her chest.

No! Please no!

She heard the first knife wing toward her and the sudden startling whap as the blade sank into the wood.

The sweat went cold on her face.

And then another whizzed by and she heard the whap as it sank in near her foot. Her knees shook.

Her head felt smoky. She was in a hazy dream. His words snaked back through her ears. "Don't decide to scratch your head or shoo a fly or wipe your nose."

Was this true, or was it a trick, the way Miss Holland's lessons had been?

She was afraid to close her eyes. Afraid to open them. One blink, one wrong breath could result in a blade through her arm, her ribs, or even her heart. She counted tick tock, tick tock, like a clock. But each time a knife gripped the board, her teeth chattered and her hands shook.

She couldn't breathe evenly. She couldn't breathe at all. A gasp lodged in her throat.

A blade buzzed by her ear.

Her head swum. Her knees felt like mush. If she moved, she would be sliced in two. A knife would separate her head from her body. It would impale her.

She closed her eyes. Memories came in a blinding rush: Papa playing the harmonica when she was a little girl. Dilly learning her times tables. Mama's face when she realized her new husband, Thomas Slater, was not who she thought he was.

Finally the whizzing stopped.

Lucy's eyes popped open. Knives were stuck deep into the wood, forming an outline of her body. A knife pulled at her hair.

"Left hand is off," Diavolo growled, pulling out each knife and throwing it on the ground with an angry clank. "Focus, Diavolo!" he shouted.

"Again," he barked. "I need more accuracy before we start the spin."

The spin?

A sickening feeling came over her. He was going to throw the knives while she spun on the wooden circle! She would be his moving target.

Lucy's hands held the handles so tightly, they ached when she let go. She leaned down to unbuckle her ankles, her fingers stiff and clumsy, the pancakes and sausages from breakfast surging up into her throat.

"Stop!" Diavolo roared.

Lucy leapt off the stand, her knees buckling underneath her, but she caught herself.

"You can't leave. You're my target girl!" he shouted.

Lucy ran like she'd never run before, the words spinning in her head.

I am no one's target girl.

CHAPTER SIXTEEN

GLITTERING SPARKS OF LIGHT

Her head hurt. She breathed in the sickening smell of puke and tried to brush off the globs of pancakes stuck to the sequins and jewels.

But all she could think was: she had made an enemy of Diavolo!

She ran back to his dressing tent and grabbed her old orphanage dress, sticking the precious paper and pencil inside.

The gong sounded. People thronged to the cook tent. Lucy threaded through the crowd in the opposite direction, heading for the elephant house.

Lucy ran around by the riverbank, where there were fewer people. She stood out in the sequined dress. She loved the shoes, though. It felt so good to run in shoes that fit.

When she got to the elephant house, she slowed down. She

could hear the scrape of shovels next door in the camel house, but the elephant house was quiet. Grace and Doris were probably on their way to the cook tent, like most everybody else.

Baby was tethered more in the pond than out. Jenny was tied nearby. She regarded Lucy without surprise, as if she'd been waiting for her. Then she sucked water into her trunk and shot it across her back.

Lucy went into the feed room and changed into her orphanage dress. Back outside, she washed her face in the cool pond water, took the button and the silk bag out of her shoe and put them in her pocket, and did her best to clean herself up. She was just finishing when a blast of water hit her. She leapt back.

But it was only Baby. Baby sucked in another trunkful and sprayed Lucy again.

Lucy grinned. Then she noticed that Jenny's food basket had rolled out of her reach. Lucy pulled it closer to the elephant and set it right-side up. Jenny went back to eating.

Lucy waited to see if Baby would squirt her again, but she seemed content now. Had Baby wanted to tell Lucy that she needed to attend to Jenny's basket?

Grace and Doris would be back in a little while. Lucy needed to figure out what to do, but she was still too upset to think clearly.

Reading soothed her. It got her mind off her worries and helped her calm down. She looked around for a book.

Near the haystack was a small table and a canvas chair. On

top of the table was a notebook. It wasn't a book, but it was something. She pulled the chair near the elephants and began reading.

Sweat forms a line around an elephant's toenails. Jenny likes when I place a cool rag on her feet. Baby has sensitive skin. I have been applying salve to her legs twice a day, she read, when suddenly an old cabbage plopped onto Lucy's lap. Lucy handed the cabbage back to Baby, who wrapped her trunk around it and shoved it in her mouth. Then her trunk found Lucy's face.

The elephant wanted something. What was it?

They had food and water. The chain that tied one foot of Baby's and one of Jenny's did not seem too tight.

Lucy went back to reading. *Elephants respond to kindness. You will never get them to do their best work, unless they trust you.* This made her think about Mackinac, Grundy, and Miss Holland. She could cross out "elephant" and write in "orphan" and give the notebook to them.

Now a carrot hurtled through the air and landed on Lucy's foot. Baby again.

Lucy offered the carrot to Jenny. Jenny wrapped her trunk around it and put it in her mouth.

Baby waded closer and Lucy went back to reading, but no sooner had she begun than she was hit by another cabbage.

Baby didn't want her to read?

Across the way a cat leapt onto the fence. It was just the four of them. Jenny, Baby, Lucy, and the cat.

Lucy's eyes lingered on the tight words handwritten in

blue. These were Grace's elephant training notes. They were important.

Lucy began reading, " 'Respect is key to the relationship,' " but this time the words went into her mind and came out her mouth.

The sound of her own voice startled her. She stopped.

Baby sent a carrot flying her way.

There was no mistaking what Baby wanted now. She wanted to hear Lucy read. Lucy began again. " 'Respect goes two ways.' "

Her voice sounded strange and deeply familiar.

Jenny got more carrots, shoving them into her mouth, the crunch deep and satisfying.

" 'Unless you first win an animal's friendship, they cannot be trained. Wild and dangerous as elephants are, you must always respect them.' "

Lucy's hands trembled, but she read on and Baby stopped throwing food. Lucy had figured out what the little elephant wanted. She kept reading as if she were in a trance. It was just Lucy and the elephants. No one else could hear.

A few minutes later she heard footsteps approaching. She leapt up, knocking the chair over, ran to the table, and returned the notebook. She said a silent goodbye to Jenny and Baby and slipped down to the river, drawn by the rushing sound. She found a large, smooth rock on the bank and sat down to think.

Betts had been nice. Maybe she would take Lucy on?

Diavolo said Betts needed someone more experienced. And Diavolo was Betts's boss. He was everyone's boss. If he hated her, he wouldn't let anyone give her an apprenticeship.

She could hide in the train. But it would be five days until they left. And where was the train, anyway?

The map at Jabo's didn't have the train. Or maybe it did and she hadn't noticed it. She'd go back and look. Jabo would be there. He'd know what to do.

She ran back around by the horse corrals and out to his train car, hoping no one would tell Diavolo where she was. He was the owner. He could force her to be his target girl.

Jabo's train car was empty. She headed straight for the map to see where the train was.

She wanted to wait for Jabo, but she didn't dare. Jabo's home would be the first place Diavolo would look.

Lucy was headed down the stairs when she spotted Nico and Jabo.

"Here she is!" Nico sprinted toward her.

"Indeed," Jabo said. "Come. Let's sit inside, shall we? We have some significant matters to discuss."

One look at their faces and Lucy knew they knew what had happened. Probably everybody knew by now.

She followed them back inside. Jabo sighed when he sat down in his upholstered arm chair, kicking his legs onto the footrest. Nico pulled up the workbench. He sat on one end, Lucy on the other.

Jabo wiped his forehead with his handkerchief. "You, my dear, have had quite the morning."

Lucy nodded.

"Diavolo dedicated three hours to training you to be his target girl. And now he's furious. I'm afraid Diavolo takes offense easily and often. And some of the roustabouts who work for him are not as refined as one would wish. They are, well . . . the word *brute* comes to mind," Jabo said.

Lucy wrote quickly, then handed her paper to Jabo.

I didn't know he was a knife thrower.

Jabo nodded. "That occurred to me. Even so, I'm wondering if this unfortunate situation could have been averted if you had been better able to communicate with him."

He wanted me because I don't speak, Lucy wrote.

"Ah, of course." Jabo made a clicking noise. "Thank you, by the way, for your letter, Lucy. I'm sorry I have not had an opportunity to respond until now."

Lucy nodded.

"You have a well-reasoned argument and an impressive facility with the written word. However, I'm not convinced that your silence is in your best interest. I believe it is a way of limiting yourself that you will soon outgrow."

Lucy frowned.

"If you don't believe me, look at the stars." Jabo pointed to the window.

What stars? It was the middle of the afternoon.

"Go look," Jabo said.

Lucy went to the window and peered up at the blue sky and the fluffy white clouds.

Jabo came up next to her. "You don't see any, do you?"

Lucy shook her head.

"I can't see them either," Jabo admitted. "But they are there waiting for the cloak of night. And then we will see them shining brilliant, luminous. Glittering sparks of light in the dark sky."

Lucy cocked her head.

"I see your voice just as clearly," Jabo whispered. "It's a star inside you waiting to shine."

Lucy bit her lip, shaking her head. He didn't understand. Not speaking kept her safe.

"I'm not the only one who believes this," Jabo said. "Bernadette said much the same thing to me, and Grace is coming around, Lucy," Jabo said. "She heard you reading to Baby."

"Out loud?" Nico asked.

Jabo nodded. "Quite unusual to have that little elephant take a liking to someone that way. Baby did not much care for Doris. The feeling, as I understand it, was mutual." Lucy exchanged a look with Nico as Jabo went on. "Made a terrible racket anytime she came near. Doris was happy to make an exit with all her limbs intact."

"After that she went to the candy butchers. They caught her stealing spun sugar," Nico said.

Jabo nodded. "Lost a chance for that, I'm afraid. She's trying for an acrobat apprenticeship, which I do not recommend. An acrobat apprentice must be able to cook an omelet while balancing on the high wire." He sighed. "If only life were long enough for all the practice that's required."

"I thought she wanted to be a fortune-teller," Nico said.

Jabo shrugged. "Socorro would have nothing to do with her. She said the crystal ball began to boil when Doris came near. But back to you, my dear. We must deal with the problem at hand. Diavolo's taken two of your chances."

Lucy gasped. All of her chances were gone!

"He can't take two for one mistake," Nico said.

"I'm afraid he can. That is an owner's prerogative."

"I have two chances left. Lucy can have one of mine," Nico said.

"That is most gracious of you, young sir. However, the chance system doesn't operate in that manner. Still, all is not lost. Betts took a liking to you, Lucy. She wishes she could take you on, but in her current condition she needs a fully trained dressmaker. Still, she wanted you to have this." Jabo handed her a flour sack.

Lucy stuck her hand inside and pulled out a blue dress, with its own blue belt! She went to the bathroom to put it on.

The dress fit perfectly. She couldn't stop looking at herself in the tiny mirror over the sink. She hadn't had a dress made for her in five years.

Jabo nodded appreciatively when she came out. "Betts is a maestra with a needle and thread. Now, I'll see that Diavolo gets the costume back, but you should wash it first."

Lucy nodded.

"All in all, you OOFOs are making good progress. Eugene is working for Nitty-Bitty. Nico has an opportunity before him. He is deciding what kind of a man he wants to be."

What did that mean?

Nico's cheeks flushed like someone had walked in on him with his undershirt on.

"And you"—Jabo looked at Lucy—"you must try again with Grace. She has agreed to take another look at you, provided you demonstrate your verbal proficiency. That's a reasonable request, my lady. She needs to know you can warn her if something goes wrong."

Lucy plunked down on the workbench and crossed her arms.

"Two words," Jabo said, his voice kind and gentle. "If you can read out loud, you can say two words."

"I'll write them down for you," Nico chimed in. "You can practice by reading 'John Robinson.'"

"That's my man, Nico."

Lucy bit the inside of her cheek, struggling to control the rising fear.

"Listen to me, Lucy," Jabo whispered. "None of us gets long on this lush and lovely planet. Don't relinquish any more of your precious life to whoever it is who has hurt you."

What was he talking about? It was her choice not to talk. Lucy turned away.

"My father measured six feet three inches. Do you know how tall I am?" Jabo asked.

Lucy shook her head.

"Three feet six inches. Six three, three six . . . nature's little joke, but it wasn't funny to me. When my father looked at me, the shame in his eyes was excruciating. The day he left me was the worst and best day of my life. I know it's not easy what we're asking of you. But look at me, Lucy."

Lucy's eyes flickered to Jabo's.

"There are people who love you. People here and people in your life before. Pretend you're talking to them. Let your voice be heard."

February 4, 1939
Home for Friendless Children
Riverport, Iowa

Dear Mrs. Mackinac,

I do not understand what you mean when you say your orphans don't remember about their lives before & that is for the best.

I don't know about your other girls, but my Lucy is smart. She would not forget she had a mama and a papa, may they rest in peace, & a big sister (me) who wants her more than any other thing in the world.

Please could you ask if any of your girls is named Lucy with a sister named Dilly, then when my Lucy raises her hand, you can send her to me. I know you say it is difficult to keep track of your girls, but my Lucy will never forget she's a Sauvé.

If you do this, there will be one less orphan to worry all about, one less orphan to feed. Please could you help me find my sister?

Yours truly,
Dilly Sauvé

February 18, 1939
Home for Friendless Children
Riverport, Iowa

Dear Mrs. Mackinac,

It is not possible that I'm mistaken about
Lucy going to your orphanage. I know my mama's
handwriting. I know the kind of paper she wrote
on & how she put one word next to another. My
mama's letter said Lucy was at the Home for Friendless
Children. Mama would not make a mistake about this.

If she is not at the Home for Friendless Children,
then when did she leave and where did she go? You
must know the name of each child at your orphanage,
when they arrived, how long they stayed & where they
went after. If you could search your records for Lucy
with the red hair, Lucy Sauvé, then I will know where
to look next.

It is more important than any other thing in the
world that I find her. If you've ever had a sister, you'll
know how I feel.

Yours truly,
Dilly Sauvé

February 22, 1939

Dear Lucy,

Remember how I picked you up at school
every day & brought you an apple slice with
cinnamon? Remember how Mama would sew us
new dresses from our old ones and we would laugh
when people said how beautiful our dresses were.
They thought we had $$ because of Mama's clever
hands.

I would do anything to talk to someone
who remembers the things that happened to us.
I can tell stories about our life to the girls in
the sewing shop, but that's not the same. When
I tell them, it's like looking through a window
at a warm fireplace. But when I write to you, we
are both sitting together warming our hands on
the fire.

Our life was not fancy when it was just you,
Mama, and me. But I didn't know how happy we were
back then. I didn't know how easy it would be for our
lives to fall apart.

Mrs. Sokoloff says I'm supposed to be a
mensch, which is Yiddish for a person who does
good. She says a mensch would forgive Thomas Slater
for what he did to us. But how do you forgive

someone who doesn't think he did even one thing wrong?

Where are you, Lucy? I don't know where to look anymore.

Love,

Dilly

CHAPTER SEVENTEEN

"THE WRONGEST POSSIBLE SIDE OF DIAVOLO"

Jabo was mistaken. Lucy's quiet was an important part of her. The elephants liked her this way. The problem was people. Jabo and Grace needed to get used to Lucy. She would need to convince them. That was all.

Lucy dunked the sparkly dress in the washbasin while Nico filled her in on what he'd learned. Diavolo was the only one of the three owners who traveled with the circus. He wasn't liked by most of the Saachi folks, but he had a knack for finding talent. The person who really ran Saachi's was his wife, Seraphina. And Seraphina had a special place in her heart for Jabo.

Lucy worked the small bits of barf from between the sparkles and baubles and scrubbed the bottom with cold sudsy water.

She wiped her hand on a towel, took out her paper and wrote. *Can Diavolo get rid of me?*

Nico's head seesawed back and forth. "He thinks he already has."

Lucy nodded and Nico continued, "After the performance on Sunday, they'll pack the train and make their first jump to Blue Creek. We'll go with them, if we have apprenticeships."

If we don't?

"We get left behind."

You?

"Me too," Nico said.

Lucy shook her head and wrote, *Your apprenticeship?*

"Oh, my apprenticeship? Dunno," he mumbled, averting his gaze.

Lucy touched his chest with her soapy finger.

Nico looked everywhere except at her.

Maybe he didn't want her to know what he was trying for in case he failed. Or maybe he was having trouble deciding what to try for.

Lucy rinsed the dress in the bathroom sink, then wrung the water out of it and hung it next to Jabo's small trousers on one of the clotheslines behind the train cars.

She wasn't sure what to do about Nico. But her next step was clear. She had to win over Grace.

At supper, Lucy headed for the roustabout table. "How's my favorite OOFO?" Bunk said as the waiter set a plate of chicken, corn on the cob, and biscuits in front of her.

Lucy sighed with pleasure.

Rib and Bunk laughed.

Lucy buttered a biscuit, keeping an eye out for Diavolo.

"Seem a little nervous, kiddo," Bunk whispered.

Lucy nodded.

"No apprenticeship yet," Rib guessed.

"Got on the wrongest possible side of Diavolo," Nevada whispered.

"Is there a right side?" Rib asked.

"But Baby took a liking to her." Bunk winked at Lucy.

"Baby," Rib groaned.

"Kind of embarrassing when an elephant is smarter than you, Rib," Bunk said.

"Smarter than the performers. Baby learns her act faster than they do," Rib said as Nico and Doris joined their table.

Bunk spun his corn cob under his butter knife. "Nico, my man, did you find the advance man's office?"

Nico nodded, his eyes on his plate.

"Get your telegram sent?" Bunk asked.

"Telegram? Who'd you send a telegram to?" Doris asked, unrolling her silverware.

Nico stuck his biscuit in his pocket. "Frank and Alice," he mumbled.

Lucy frowned.

Doris's eyes bulged. Her fork froze in the air. "Why?"

"Tell them where I am," Nico whispered.

Doris got a forkful of chicken. "Frank and Alice don't care."

"Now, now, Miss Doris. You leave Nico alone. We love who we love," Bunk said.

"You didn't meet Frank and Alice," Doris said.

Lucy had to agree with Doris. She didn't know how Nico could still care about Frank and Alice.

"Did Frank telegram back?" Doris asked.

Nico straightened up. "Yes."

"What'd he say?" Doris asked.

"They can't come. They're busy."

Doris raised her eyebrows at Bunk as if that proved her point.

Bunk shrugged.

"I'll tell you what," Rib said, "I heard Nico practicing his grind. The boy has a gift."

Lucy didn't know what a grind was, but by the time she wrote her question, the conversation would have moved on. Her way of communicating didn't work well in a group. People didn't pay attention to the expression on her face. People's eyes followed the person who did the talking. Nobody waited for her to write.

Nico's eyes lit up. "Want to hear?" he asked.

"Course we do," Bunk said.

Nico wiped his mouth, pasted on the sleek mustache Jabo had given him, and stood up. "Ladies and gentlemen," his voice rang out, "inside are sights and sounds beyond your wildest imaginings. There are men so tall they can reach upstairs without climbing a single step and women who can ride two horses at the same time. Ladies fly through the air held by ribbons. Horses perform ballet on two legs." The words slid out of his mouth as if they'd been buttered on both sides.

Now Lucy understood. A grind was a word song that made you want to buy a ticket. Lucy grinned at Nico. His eyes glowed at her approval.

"I'd say you have a future here, my man." Bunk nodded to Nico. "And Eugene's certainly found a sweet spot."

"Very sweet," Rib agreed.

"He came to us," Bunk said, "but the boy smelled like corn bread. Pretty clear where he belonged."

"Never hurts to have a friend in the pie car," Rib said.

"Never does," Nevada agreed.

"Well, I'm going to be an acrobat," Doris announced.

Bunk and Rib exchanged a worried look.

"I haven't lost all my chances the way she has." Doris directed her thumb at Lucy.

"Got to get her talking is all," Bunk said.

"Let's tickle her," Rib said as Diavolo and Seraphina swept by. Lucy slid under the table.

"Where'd she go?" Rib asked.

Lucy waited for Diavolo and Seraphina to take their places at the head table, then she crawled back onto the bench. She had just swallowed the last bite of biscuit when Diavolo returned with Jabo in tow.

"I thought we had agreed your OOFOs only get three chances," Diavolo said, his eye on Lucy.

"Yes, sir." Jabo nodded. "But there are extenuating circumstances. Special talents, if you will."

Diavolo crossed his arms. "Either we have rules or we don't."

"Ordinarily I'd agree with you, but . . ."

"She wasted my entire morning, Jabo. I find her on the train and I'll have her red-lighted. Am I making myself clear?" Diavolo asked.

"She's only a child. I really don't think—" Jabo said, but it was too late. Diavolo was already gone.

CHAPTER EIGHTEEN

"First-of-Mays"

"**W**hat does 'red-lighted' mean?" Nico asked Jabo when they were back in Jabo's home.

"It means you're asked to leave the train in a rather primitive fashion. You're left on the tracks watching the red lights of the caboose as it pulls away. Kicked off, if you will. But, Lucy, don't despair. Grace will come around." Jabo pulled on a fresh pair of striped socks. "Still, I think it only prudent that you stay out of the cook tent until you get squared away. Eugene, can you make sure Lucy gets meal baskets sent here?"

"Yes, sir," Eugene said. Eugene was the only one of the four of them who had an apprenticeship for sure. Nitty-Bitty had given him a route card, which listed where the circus would be going and when. You only got that if you had a secure place on the train. After Eugene got his route card, he stood straighter and smiled more often, and the aroma of chocolate followed him wherever he went. Lucy watched him wistfully.

Jabo nodded. "You're a good man, Eugene."

"I need my costume by seven tomorrow," Doris whined. "And you were wrong about these." She tossed the red clown noses on to Jabo's bed. "I don't want them."

Jabo ran a comb though his hair. "Let's not put our tigers before our elephants, Mademoiselle Doris. Nobody auditions in a costume."

"Well, I am. You said you were gonna help me." Doris glared at him.

"I'm doing my best, my dear. But it isn't reasonable to believe you'll be chosen for an acrobatic apprenticeship without—"

"My hair is growing!" Doris stamped her foot.

"Your hair poses no problem." Jabo set his comb down. "It's practice you're lacking. Years of it, I'm afraid."

Doris frowned. "Well," she huffed, "I can always work in the cook tent. *That* isn't hard."

Jabo pursed his lips. "First, there isn't room in the pie car for two apprentices. But more importantly, it is unbecoming, undignified, and uncharitable to demean the skills of a fellow OOFO—your brother, as I understand."

Doris shrugged. "Eugene can convince Nitty to take me on, can't you, Eugene?"

Eugene said nothing. Jabo shook his head.

* * *

149

The next morning when Lucy woke up, she saw the breakfast basket Eugene had brought for her. She pulled back the checkered napkin and discovered sugar-shake donuts warm from the fryer and a mason jar of apple sauce.

Jabo had gotten Eugene right. He was an ace in the hole.

Lucy wanted to thank him, but he was already gone. Only Nico was here.

"Thought I'd walk you to the elephant house," he said.

After a quick breakfast they headed to Water Street, passing white horses, a clown, and a lady on stilts carrying birdcages in each hand.

Everyone was in a hurry, the air buzzing with excitement, like the orphanage on Christmas Eve when the girls would each get a small bag of Christmas candy. The first performance of the season was just four days away, and then the entire circus would be loaded onto train cars. The train would be their home for the next five months. Last year they gave performances in sixty-five towns.

There wasn't much time to win Grace over. And Lucy didn't want to think what would happen if she didn't.

When Lucy and Nico got to the river, they spotted a line of men waiting outside the camel house.

Lucy threw a questioning look at Nico.

"They're the guys who are brand-new to circus work. First-of-Mays, they're called. Grace is hiring. Bunk doesn't have much time to help with Baby. He has to supervise loading the train."

Grace sat in a canvas chair in front of the camel house. One by one the men approached, hat in hand. Lucy wished she could hear the questions Grace was asking. When the interview was done, the man would either walk away or join another line near the camel house.

Nico pointed to the second line. "Must be the guys that made it to round two."

First in line was a tall guy with green suspenders; then came a man with freckles and a cowlick. Last was a young guy with soft pink cheeks and big doughy ears.

The second stage of the interview had to be meeting Baby. That would probably happen behind the elephant house. Lucy had just written a note to Nico suggesting they move so they could see the second part of the interview, when she heard footsteps behind her.

Doris.

Oh no. What was she doing here?

"Hi," Doris whispered.

"I thought you were auditioning," Nico said.

"This afternoon."

Last night Doris had said the audition was first thing in the morning. Had the time changed? Or was she lying?

Audition? Lucy wrote.

Doris scowled at Lucy. "I just said it's this afternoon."

"You can't stay with us. Baby doesn't like you," Nico said under his breath.

Doris's eyes grew small and mean.

"If you don't get the acrobat spot, how about drummer? Musicians sit with the performers. You'll like that."

"I want to wear a pretty costume," Doris said.

"We can't promise that," Nico said.

"Well, what can you promise?" Doris asked.

Nico and Lucy exchanged a look.

"I hate when you do that," Doris said.

"Do what?" Nico asked.

"Have a private conversation."

"We didn't say a word."

"You know what I mean." Doris scratched her scalp. "You even nod like you have secrets."

"Look, we're trying to help you," Nico said.

"It doesn't seem like it," Doris growled. "All of us or none of us, remember?"

Nico nodded.

Doris's eyes found Lucy's. Her face softened. "You owe me a song."

Lucy crossed her two pointer fingers and moved them to her heart—the sign of the orphan swear.

Doris made the sign back.

"Okay, I'm leaving. I know Baby doesn't like me. Just don't forget you promised to sing," Doris whispered to Lucy, and then she slipped away.

Lucy and Nico stole around the side of the elephant house to where Baby was splashing in the watering hole and Jenny was rocking from foot to foot. Grace's big dog, Tiny, was sitting on an elephant stand watching the elephants, as if he were on guard duty. Lucy and Nico ran behind the hay bales and shifted them until a small hole opened so they could see. Then they settled down to wait for Grace. A few minutes later she made her way around the pond, the first-of-Mays following.

When Baby saw Grace, she splashed over to the side of the water hole and reached her trunk out.

"Hi, Baby," Grace cooed.

The little elephant lumbered toward her.

"Say hello, Baby," Grace said.

Baby lifted one foot in the air, and flipped it up and down like a wave.

Grace offered her a sugar cube. Baby set her foot down, picked up the cube with her trunk, and fed it to her mouth. Lucy marveled at how delicate an elephant's trunk was—it could pick up a tiny sugar cube. But it was strong, too. Lucy had seen Grace stand on Jenny's trunk.

Grace had the men stand in a line facing Baby.

"Okay, Baby, you decide," Grace called, and Baby made a beeline for the freckly guy, her trunk burrowing into his pocket.

"You got food in there?" Grace called.

The freckly guy tried to bat Baby away. "No, ma'am."

But Baby had found an apple. She popped the apple into her mouth, crunching happily.

"You are excused, sir," Grace called out.

"Why?" the freckly guy asked.

153

"Did I ask you if you had food?"

He nodded.

"And what did you say?"

"That's not food. It's my dinner," he grumbled, turning to leave. Baby followed. And the freckly guy began to hurry. Baby trotted. He broke into a run.

"Stop, Baby!" Grace shouted, and the elephant came to a halt, her eyes on Grace.

Grace beckoned and Baby came back to her.

"Anybody else have food?" Grace barked to the other first-of-Mays.

"No, ma'am." Suspenders and Pink Cheeks shook their heads. But Suspenders was creeping backward. "You got other work, ma'am? Don't think I want to mess with a half-crazy elephant."

Grace nodded. "Go check with Bunk," she said. Then she turned her attention to Pink Cheeks.

"Your dad worked at Hagenbeck-Wallace?"

"Yes, ma'am," Pink Cheeks said.

Grace nodded. "All right, then. Baby, what do you think?"

Baby walked forward with her trunk pointed out. But she didn't stop by Pink Cheeks. She continued around the haystack to Nico and Lucy.

Lucy grinned, but when Grace came around the haystack, she wasn't smiling. "No, Lucy. We've been through this before. Baby is voice trained. You need to be able—"

"Jabo said you might be willing to give her a chance," Nico interrupted.

"Jabo doesn't work in the menagerie and he's not my boss," Grace snarled.

Pink Cheeks swaggered up. "If you don't mind me saying, miss, you have to let them elephants know who's the boss."

"Is that so?" Grace asked.

"Yes, miss," Pink Cheeks said.

"But Baby doesn't seem to care for you," Grace said.

"The way I was taught, that ain't important. Elephants got to know you mean business. You got to make them pay, if they don't. That's the way they did it at Hagenbeck."

"Well . . . that's not the way we do it here. You're excused," Grace said.

"*I'm* excused?" Pink Cheeks snorted. "Who thought it was a good idea to put a lady in charge?"

"Say goodbye, Baby," Grace commanded, and Baby bent one leg and bowed to Pink Cheeks.

With Pink Cheeks gone, Grace eyed Lucy. "I'm not taking you on, so don't go getting your hopes up. I could use some help this morning. That's all."

Thank you! Lucy flashed her page.

Grace locked eyes with Lucy. "I won't communicate with you that way. Do you understand?"

Lucy nodded. She understood. She just didn't agree.

CHAPTER NINETEEN

VOCABULARY LIST

Lucy spent the next four days washing buckets, scrubbing stands, shining harnesses, polishing headdresses, and raking up colossal piles of elephant poop. She worked inside the barn when the elephants were outside, and outside the barn when the elephants were inside.

During that time, Nico worked as Jabo's right-hand man and Eugene became so important to Nitty-Bitty, it seemed like he had always worked there. Doris, on the other hand, upset the unicyclists, alienated the aerialists, and got banned from the horse barn. Eugene had tried to explain to Doris that the way to get a spot was to know what a boss wanted even before he or she did. Doris shrugged off his advice, but Lucy wanted more.

Should I get to the elephant barn earlier than Grace? she wrote.

Eugene nodded. "But don't get near the elephants until she comes."

Should I polish her boots?

"Ask her first."

When should I ask if she'll take me on?

Eugene thought about this a long while before answering. "Not until the last day. Let her get used to depending on you," he said.

Lucy knew Grace adored her elephants, had a soft spot for Bunk, and liked the barn clean as a kitchen. Lucy loved the elephants and Bunk, but keeping the big barn as clean as Grace wanted was challenging. Still, she tried her best to follow Grace's instructions.

But by Sunday morning, Grace still hadn't brought up the apprenticeship. Lucy had written her a letter to make her case, but Grace had refused to read it.

Lucy was up on the road dumping a wheelbarrow load near a sign that read FARMERS: FREE ELEPHANT DUNG! when she heard the midday meal gong.

She set the shovel into the wheelbarrow, where it rattled and bumped as she ran back to the barn. When she got inside, Grace was slipping off her coveralls to reveal slim black pants underneath. At the circus some women wore pants like men did. Lucy wondered what Mama would have said about that. "Go on to the cook tent. Be back in half an hour." Grace hung the overalls on a hook and went out.

Grace hadn't noticed that Lucy didn't go to the cook tent. Nor had she said a word about Diavolo. Was it possible Grace didn't know Diavolo wanted to red light Lucy?

Lucy sprayed down the cement. She was winding the hose back onto its wall hook when Nico set the dinner basket on the hay bale.

"I got it!" he gasped, breathing hard from the run. "I'm outside talker and Jabo is ringmaster!"

Lucy hugged Nico. Nico hugged her back, rocking her off her heels and swinging her around. He danced her around the small pond, Lucy's ponytail bobbing, her feet following Nico's lead. They were sailing past the elephants when Lucy spotted Doris.

"Lucy likes Nico! Lucy likes Nico," Doris sang.

Lucy's arms dropped to her sides, stiff as broom handles. She grabbed a rake and set to work, her face flushed.

Nico's ears were red and his foot shook. "Shut up, Doris," he muttered.

"You like her, too. Everyone knows you do," Doris said.

Nico turned on the hose and washed his hands. "Are you eating with us?" he asked.

"I'm going to the cook tent. I'm sitting on the performers' side. You ought to come and see," Doris said.

"You got an apprenticeship?"

"I did!" Doris beamed.

Lucy dropped the rake and hugged Doris.

Nico gave her his best bow. "Where?" he asked.

"Performer, like I just said!" Doris bragged. "But not a clown!"

Nico nodded. "You get a route card?"

"I'm going to. I am!"

"Who gave you the apprenticeship?"

"Come to the cook tent and you'll see."

Nico pulled sandwiches out of the basket. "We can't. You know that."

Doris stood watching him, her hands on her hips. "The food's better at the cook tent."

Nico shrugged. "We have an extra sandwich, if you want to join us."

"I don't. Obviously." Doris scowled. She waited, hoping he would change his mind. When he didn't, she stomped off.

Lucy put the rake away and washed her hands.

"Who do you suppose took her on?" Nico asked.

Lucy shrugged.

"If she got a spot, you definitely will. Grace is going to take you on. Eugene said he asked Nitty to talk to her about it."

Eugene was a good friend. He and Nico both looked out for her.

Nico chewed his sandwich, then wiped his mouth. "Jabo is so excited, he can't stop talking. He'll be the only dwarf

ringmaster in America. 'Today is a big day for little people,'"
Nico said, imitating Jabo.

Lucy laughed.

Nico polished his apple with his shirt tail. "And"—he stole
a quick look at her—"I got a route card! I'm the outside talker.
then I change into my costume and stand by Jabo during the
performance. I'm his right-hand man!"

Can I see? Lucy wrote.

Nico took the card out of his pocket and handed it to Lucy
with a grand flourish. On the top it said "Saachi's Circus Spectacular" with a picture of Diavolo in his white shirt and red silk
vest and Seraphina in a jeweled headdress. Below were two col-
umns with dates on one side, cities and railroads on the other.

Lucy ran her finger over the card. They all had apprenticeships except her.

"You'll get yours. You will," Nico said. Then they heard
Grace's heavy boot steps approaching. Lucy handed back
the card.

Nico left Lucy the extra sandwich, grabbed the empty
basket, and slipped away.

A minute later, Grace appeared wearing a stretchy costume with burgundy beads, her hair braided and pinned on
top of her head.

Lucy helped Grace fit a burgundy beaded headdress on
Jenny. Then Grace got Baby out of the pond. "Don't let her lie
down," Grace barked, handing Lucy a towel.

How were you supposed to keep nine hundred pounds of willful elephant from lying down?

Baby liked being dried off. She wiggled her bottom against the towel and lifted one leg for Lucy to wipe behind it. Then she looped her trunk around the towel and waved it in the air.

Grace tethered Baby and took the towel from her. "Can you keep an eye on Baby until Bunk gets here? Don't let her back in the pond."

Lucy nodded, a thrill traveling through her. This was more responsibility than Grace had given her before. It was a good sign.

After Grace left, Lucy found the training book and began reading to Baby, but Baby wasn't in a reading mood. Baby wanted to play.

Lucy took a handful of apples and began rolling them to the little elephant. Baby seized one and stuck it in her mouth. Lucy rolled another. Then another.

Baby liked this game, but she wasn't happy when the apples were all gone.

Baby stepped forward.

Lucy stepped backward.

Forward.

Backward.

Forward.

Backward until Lucy's back was jammed against the barn wall. Baby's trunk pushed at her chest insistently.

Lucy's heart began to beat too fast. If Baby took another step forward, she'd crush Lucy's foot.

But Baby wanted another apple.

Lucy dug in her pocket and pulled out her vocabulary list and offered that to Baby. While the little elephant was trying to pick it out of Lucy's hand, Lucy slipped by her.

Baby stuck the paper in her mouth, then swallowed.

"Lucy," Bunk barked, startling Lucy.

Lucy jumped.

"Don't let her get the best of you," Bunk said.

Lucy nodded. She was glad Grace hadn't seen this.

"What did you give her, anyway?"

Vocabulary list, Lucy wrote.

"You don't think she's smart enough already?" Bunk asked.

They were still laughing when Grace appeared. "Nice of you to show up," she told Bunk.

"It *was* nice of me," Bunk said. "I stay on your good side. You could break me in half like a toothpick."

"I could," Grace agreed, "but then who would load the train?"

"So I'm safe until the train is loaded? Good to know," Bunk said.

"Yes," Grace agreed with a sly smile. Then she turned to Lucy. "You're to stay with Bunk and help him with Baby. Fill your pockets with sugar cubes, but never reward her unless she's followed your command. Baby is the smartest animal I've ever worked with. She always has a plan. We have to make sure she puts our plans before her plans."

Lucy nodded. Baby had a mind of her own. No doubt about that.

"Come on, I'll show you what I mean," Grace said.

Grace positioned Lucy with her back to Baby's trunk. Then she picked up a giant hairbrush and handed it to the elephant. Baby wound her trunk around the brush and began sending the bristles down through Lucy's ponytail. Lucy giggled. If she closed her eyes, she could almost imagine Dilly brushing her hair.

"Now give her the sugar cube," Grace commanded.

Baby whisked the sugar cube out of Lucy's hand, stuck it in her mouth, and crunched happily.

"She's proud of herself when she does a good job."

Grace fit a white felt beret on Baby's head and elephant-size bloomers on her two front legs. The smock went on last. *Parisian Coiffeuse Elephantoff* was stitched across the back; on the front: *Baby.*

Jenny lowered her head and Grace climbed on her trunk; then Jenny raised her head and Grace slipped onto her back.

"Time to move out," Grace called when the bugle trilled. She and Jenny took the lead. Baby walked behind with Lucy and Bunk.

In the distance, Lucy could see townie kids perched on a fence staring at them the way the girls at the orphanage did when you still had Christmas candy left and they had eaten theirs.

A week ago she was shoveling sand into bags at the orphanage, and now here she was a circus girl, with kids looking at her enviously.

Anyway, she had an apprenticeship now. She'd watched Baby all by herself. That was an elephant girl's job.

CHAPTER TWENTY

ELEPHANTOFF

They headed into the big top to a staging area where Seraphina stood with her clipboard. Tiny the Great Dane pranced in the sawdust wearing an elephant costume. A roustabout had to fix his cummerbund when it came undone.

"Tiny follows Jenny in the spec. The spec is the first act, but don't call it the first act or you'll sound like a first-of-May," Bunk explained.

Grace found them a spot to stand behind the band pit. She and Bunk got Baby settled; then Lucy turned to watch the backstage action.

"Where are the aerialists?" Seraphina called.

A clown bent over his small car, a giant wrench in his hand. Lions paced back and forth in gold cages. A herd of white liberty horses with flowing manes trotted by.

Grace looked down at Lucy from her perch on Jenny's back. "I'll be back as soon as I'm done with the strong-woman act. Bunk will be with you the whole time, right Bunk?"

"Yes, ma'am," Bunk said.

"If Baby gets scared, calm her with your voice," Grace began, then caught herself. "Oh, Lucy," she groaned. "What am I going to do with you?"

Lucy's stomach began to hurt.

I can do this. I can do this. I can do this!

The words circled her head but didn't go near her mouth.

Lucy peeked over the musicians' gold-tasseled hats to the center of the ring, where Nico and Jabo stood on a raised platform wearing matching black top hats, red jackets, and tall black boots. Nico wore his mustache. Jabo held the microphone in his hand.

The brass section boomed in Lucy's ears. The spec was just beginning. White horses galloped with riders standing on their backs. Then came camels pulling a carriage, a man with snakes wrapped around his head, and ladies riding zebras. Somehow the staging area sorted itself into a spectacular parade of performances in the ring.

Baby was transfixed. She watched everything as if she'd paid for a ticket. When the spec was over, Grace tied up Jenny, then ducked into the women's dressing room. A moment later she came out wearing a flowery dress with a white lace collar and a big straw hat. Three women with the same hats and dresses followed her.

All four of them ran out to the raised platform in the center of the ring.

"The strongest woman ever to stand on this earth," Jabo's voice thundered across the big top. "How did she get this strong? Ladies, you know the answer . . . housework! Yes, ordinary housework, everyday chores. There's no telling the power of you fine females in the audience today. How many of you can carry your man with one arm? Don't be shy, ladies. Raise your hand."

The crowd roared with laughter.

"Of course you can! And like you, Lady Grace never loses her femininity, her graciousness, her charm. Watch how she serves tea."

There was Grace, carrying one woman on her shoulders and another on her left arm. The drum rolled and the third woman hopped on a springboard and sailed through the air onto the shoulders of the woman on Grace's shoulders.

Grace staggered, then caught herself as she walked haltingly to the tea table. With two straw-hatted women on her back and another on her left arm, Grace poured tea from a delicate teapot into china cups, each on its own saucer. Her hand shook, but her strong legs were planted as she handed each lady a cup of tea. When all the ladies had their teacups, Grace picked up the last cup and saucer and all four took a sip.

The crowd cheered.

*   *   *

When Grace returned, her face gleaming with sweat, she slipped into the dressing room and came out a minute later wearing white pants and a smock that matched Baby's.

"Next up . . . Elephantoff," Seraphina called.

In the big top, three clowns transformed the center stage into a hair salon with a painted window that read LA COIFFEUSE PARISIENNE, ELEPHANTOFF, HAIR CUTTING AND STYLING. The salon had a hooded hair dryer and a table for the oversize curling iron, comb, and hairbrush.

In the back of the shop was a mattress and a big pillow next to a small table where a candelabra had been set.

The shop door opened and Baby and Grace walked into the ring and through the door. Baby's trunk was stiff and her ears were flapping. Lucy knew that elephants flapped their ears when they were upset. But Grace spoke to Baby, and she relaxed.

"This," Jabo said, "is the amazing Elephantoff, Coiffeuse Parisienne. People wait years for an appointment in her shop. Now, Elephantoff, you must do a bit of housekeeping in your hairdresser's shop and then go to sleep so that you'll be ready to receive customers tomorrow."

Baby took the rag from Grace's hand and ran it over the table and the hair dryer.

Grace offered a sugar cube to Baby; then she trudged to the pillow.

"Now Elephantoff must get comfortable," Jabo announced.

Baby's trunk plumped the pillow then pulled a gigantic

balloon painted to look like a bug out from under it. Baby dropped the balloon bug to the ground and stomped it with her foot, making a loud pop.

Everyone laughed.

Baby stiffened. Her ears stood straight out.

Once again, Grace calmed Baby and directed her to get on the bed, lie down, and put her head on the pillow. "Good night, Elephantoff," Jabo whispered over the loudspeaker.

The lights on the shop flickered out, then flashed back on.

"Good morning, Elephantoff," Jabo said as a clown in a driver's cap led Dame Catherine, riding a white pony, into the ring. The dwarf was sitting sidesaddle, wearing her fur coat and clutching her handbag.

"You can't be late for an appointment with Elephantoff," Jabo announced, and the clown began to run. When the pony got to the shop door, Dame Catherine hopped down.

"Your appointment is here, Elephantoff," Jabo announced.

Dame Catherine walked into the shop, hung her coat on the coatrack, slipped on an *Elephantoff* smock, and climbed up in the hairdresser's chair.

Grace offered a bowl of sudsy water to Baby, who scooped up the foam with her trunk and dumped it over Catherine's head. Suds dripped down Catherine's dark hair and over her shoulders. Catherine kicked with her small legs, but Baby kept lathering until the woman was covered with great globs of shampoo.

Catherine's hands shot up. She jumped from the chair and raced to the pretend shop door. Baby ran after her.

"Madame! Madame! Elephantoff hasn't completed her work," Jabo announced, but Catherine kept running.

"Wait! Wait! You must pay!" Jabo shouted.

Grace gave a command and Baby stopped.

Then, from under her smock, Catherine pulled out a bath-towel-size dollar bill and a sugar cube, which she offered to Baby. Baby's trunk found the sugar and put it in her mouth. Then she took the giant money in her trunk and waved it in the air. The crowd went wild, clapping and cheering.

Baby, Grace, and Catherine took a bow, then the clown led the white pony back into the ring. But every time Catherine tried to mount, the clown would move the pony or boost Catherine over the top. Jabo handed the microphone to Nico and ran to help. He'd just gotten Catherine on when Seraphina called from backstage.

"Next up, unicycles!"

Grace turned Baby around and headed for the exit just as unicyclists in sparkly blue pants entered the back of the ring and began cycling around the perimeter. When Baby saw them, her legs stiffened. She trumpeted loudly and tore off in the wrong direction.

Grace chased after, calling to her.

But Baby had stopped hearing. She ran flat out for the entrance, knocking down a candy butcher and dislodging a tent pole.

The audience rose to its feet shouting and screaming. Mothers grabbed children and lunged for the stairs. Lucy took off after Baby, just as Nico's soothing voice came over the microphone. "Elephantoff has a headache. You must excuse her. She has run to the pharmacy to get an aspirin." Nico's voice carried from one end of the big top to the other, calming the crowd.

People stopped running and returned to their seats. Children giggled and clapped. Everyone was laughing and cheering for Elephantoff.

Nico had convinced the audience that this was part of the act, but Lucy knew it wasn't. Grace would never allow Baby to knock down a tent pole and run over a man.

Bunk was headed for the candy butcher to make sure the man was all right. Lucy ran around the back of the tent to help Grace catch Baby.

But when she got to the other side, Grace and Baby had disappeared.

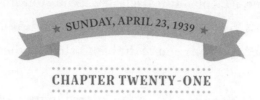

CHAPTER TWENTY-ONE

THE ELEPHANT CAR

Lucy guessed the terrified little elephant would run as far from the unicyclists as possible. She headed down the road that led away from the circus, which was quiet now. Everyone was inside the big top.

Lucy ran fast, searching for signs of Baby. Grace had said elephants loved to plunder fields and gardens. They liked to rip limbs from trees. Lucy saw a flowering tree by the side of the road, but no branches were torn off. Maybe Baby hadn't come this way.

Lucy stopped to catch her breath. She was about to turn around when she heard an elephant trumpet and she took off again. When she rounded the corner, she saw Baby charging toward a big metal gate. *Bang! Smash!* Baby thundered through, bursting the lock, popping bolts and hinges.

Once inside the train yard gate, Baby ran down the line of train cars until she got to #27, the elephant car. Then she stopped and stood obediently, as if waiting her turn to board.

Baby had had enough of Winter Quarters. She was ready to go.

Lucy caught up with her. She took a sugar cube out of her pocket, but then she remembered what Grace had said. She shouldn't reward Baby for running away.

Lucy made sure Baby saw her, then she beckoned as Grace had done.

Baby ignored Lucy, exploring the side of the train car with her trunk. Lucy motioned to Baby again, offering the sugar cube. Baby's ears flapped. Her trunk was stiff. She did not move.

Lucy beckoned again.

Still nothing.

"Calm her with your voice," Grace had said, but there was nothing to read.

Lucy looked around. No one was here yet, but they would be soon.

Then she had an idea. If she spoke in gibberish, no one would know if she misspoke.

"Vanamganham," Lucy said as calmly as she could. "Lamanaforgonna." Each made-up word was full of calming, rhythmic sounds.

Baby wavered, rocking from foot to foot. Her trunk relaxed.

Grace had said Baby must be convinced to execute your plan or she would come up with one of her own.

173

Lucy wanted Baby to walk back to Winter Quarters with her.

"Nomalomamomo." Lucy held out a sugar cube.

Baby turned to Lucy, her small brown eye watching. Lucy beckoned. "Nomalomamomo," she repeated.

Baby stopped rocking.

"Lamoofaloofa," Lucy said.

Baby took a step toward Lucy.

"Moofaloofa," Lucy said.

Now Baby was walking to Lucy. When she arrived, Lucy gave her two sugar cubes, then turned toward Winter Quarters and Baby plodded after her.

Through the train yard they went, back to the road, where Grace caught up with them.

"Thank God," Grace said, her voice aching with relief. "She get in any trouble other than the candy butcher and the tent pole?"

Lucy nodded.

Grace sighed. "Don't tell me. I don't want to know. I'll send Bunk out. He's the world's best fixer. C'mon, I'll walk you back to the elephant house. Then I have to run back to the ring for the finale."

As they grew closer, Lucy was surprised how quickly things were changing. The roustabouts were striking the menagerie tent. The cook tent canvas was lying like a great white skin on the ground. The oohs and aahs from the big top could still be heard, but much of the rest of the circus was getting packed up.

When they got back to the elephant house, Lucy had never been so glad to get anywhere. It felt like home.

Grace hadn't said anything about Lucy finding Baby and getting her to walk back to Winter Quarters, but Lucy could read approval in the woman's eyes. Lucy had proved she didn't need to speak to get the job done. Not real words, anyway.

When Baby was settled, quietly chewing leaves, Grace hurried back to the big top. Then, Lucy found the notebook and began reading.

She was halfway through the notebook when Grace and Jenny came back.

"You did well today, Lucy," Grace said, slipping off Jenny's back.

Lucy could feel the warmth in those words. She had made it. She was the elephant girl!

"I'll take you on, provided I can get you to open your mouth," Grace said.

Lucy's neck stiffened.

"Your friend Nico saved our bacon today. 'Elephantoff has a headache. She has run to the pharmacy to get an aspirin.' That was brilliant. But what if you'd been in a pinch like that?" Grace asked.

Lucy bit her lip. She wouldn't be in a pinch like that. She wasn't Jabo's apprentice.

Grace turned to her. "Just say 'John Robinson,' and the elephant girl job is yours."

Grace was bluffing. She had to have help with Baby. There was no one but Lucy. Lucy shook her head.

Grace's green eyes grew hard. "Well, then . . . thank you for your help, and good luck to you." She walked away.

Grace hadn't meant that. She would change her mind. She'd proved herself to Grace. She had!

"You heard me. Go on, get out of here," Grace called from the feed room.

Lucy stared at the feed room door. But when Grace came out, Lucy could see in the hard set of her expression that she was serious.

There was nothing to do but go.

The parking lot was empty. The horses were being herded to the train yard. An old bum clown was running with a knapsack and a Chihuahua. An acrobat sped by with hatboxes in each hand and a pillow under each arm.

Eight men were stacking rolls of canvas. Roustabouts were heaving trunks onto a truck bed. A handful of dwarfs were carrying tent stakes. An old car was jammed with pots, pans, and bags of sugar and flour.

Lucy ran back to Jabo's.

But when she got inside, his train car was empty. Nico, Eugene, Bald Doris, and all of their bedding were gone.

March 8, 1939

Dear Lucy,

"Chutzpah" is another Yiddish word Mrs. Sokoloff uses. She says it means courage.

I need courage to stand up to Mrs. Mackinac, because I have been getting all kinds of answers from her that don't make sense. First she sent a picture of another Lucy. Then she said you had never been there. Now she says Lucy with the red hair got adopted.

At Mrs. LaFinestre's shop we know how many dresses are made each day. We know how many bolts of fabric and spools of thread we use and how many finished dresses and blouses go out. We know which stores they go to and how much $$ the stores pay.

Dresses and shirts are not so important as human beings. How could there be no record of who was at the orphanage and where they went after that? And why would Mama's letter say one thing and Mrs. Mackinac's letter say another and then a different something else in the next? I need the courage to find the truth about what happened to you.

Love,
Dilly

March 8, 1939
Home for Friendless Children
Riverport, Iowa

Dear Mrs. Mackinac,

I know you have a lot of orphans to look after &
more important things to do than look through old
files. I understand how a person can be so busy she
doesn't have time at all.

I have a good idea to help out. I'm sewing dresses
at night after my work is done. I'm making extra $$,
so I can come to your orphanage & look in the files
for you.

I will let you know when I have enough $$ for
my round-trip train ticket & one way for Lucy & one
night in a boardinghouse.

Yours truly,
Dilly Sauvé

CHAPTER TWENTY-TWO

"JOHN ROBINSON"

Lucy's hands shook as she rolled her pillow into her blanket. She was running down the front steps when she spotted Doris heading her way.

"Lucy, come on!" Doris beckoned. "Our stuff is already on the train."

Lucy took off after Doris.

"I got a route card. Did you?" Doris called back.

Lucy felt tears well up.

She would have to find a way to get on without a route card. Was that even possible?

They ran all the way to the freight yard. Baskets of apples were being loaded onto the pie car. An ostrich cage was being lifted onto another car.

Behind them, roustabouts rolled a wagon carrying a tiger cage. DO NOT TOUCH: **DANGER!** WILD ANIMALS the sign said.

Lucy saw Bunk, Rib, and Nevada. She ran to Bunk and gave him a big hug.

"The OOFO likes you," Rib said.

"I'm a likable guy," Bunk agreed.

"So you say," Rib said. "But I haven't seen evidence."

Lucy was writing *Help!* when Nico appeared.

"Let's find Grace. Get you squared away," Nico said.

Lucy's face fell. She backed away, but Nico grabbed her hand and pulled her along.

A bugle trilled through the air as they ran down the line to the menagerie cars.

Roustabouts stowed ramps, shut doors. Performers shuttled the last boxes to the cars. A pile of equipment was rapidly disappearing. An entire circus had been packed in two hours.

"Forty minutes till we leave," Eugene called out.

Across the dirt road, Lucy saw Jenny with her big leather harness dragging tent poles. Grace was on her back; Baby trailed behind.

Roustabouts unhooked the tent poles and carried them down the line to a flat car. Grace whispered to Jenny; the elephant lowered her head, and the roustabout lifted the harness off.

Nico, Jabo, Nevada, Rib, Bunk, and Baby stood by the elephant car. Lucy scurried up the elephant ramp with her bedroll. She'd get all set up before Grace arrived. Grace would change her mind. She had to.

"Hold on there, cowboy." Bunk took her blankets out of her arms. "You got some business to tend to."

Lucy's face went numb.

"All you have to do is say two words. Grace wants you!" Nico whispered.

Lucy shook her head. Tears welled up again.

"Two words, Lucy. They won't let you on unless you do," Nico said.

Then Eugene appeared. "John Robinson," he whispered. "None of us wants to go without you."

They were all watching. Everybody knew what she had to do. Word traveled as fast here, as it did in the orphanage.

Why couldn't she make them understand how impossible this was?

Grace whispered to Jenny. The elephant kneeled her big front legs down, and Grace slipped off her back. Then she turned to Lucy, her voice unexpectedly gentle. "You know what to do."

"We're right here." Nico stood next to her.

"You can borrow this," Eugene whispered, slipping his ace of hearts into her hand.

Lucy's teeth chattered. She looked out at the circle of people she had grown to love.

Rib rocked back, his hand pretending to block her. "Best take cover. She's gonna blow us down with that voice of hers."

Jabo beckoned for Lucy to lean down to his level. He squeezed her hand. "Your voice is there. All you have to do is let it out."

Lucy swallowed, her mouth dry as cornmeal.

Everyone was staring. Even the people hurrying by stopped to see what was happening.

But if she opened her mouth, she opened the door to Miss Holland and Matron Mackinac inside her head.

"You think this is your family. But they're not. They'll turn on you when they hear the way you speak."

Lucy shuffled her feet. Her eyes bulged. Spit flew out of her mouth.

"You can do this," Nico said under his breath, but she could hardly hear him.

Her ears were ringing. Her feet itched to run away.

Jenny's orbiting brown eye fixed on her. The finger at the end of her long trunk nuzzled Lucy's ear and wound around her hair. Lucy's fingers touched the wrinkly hide.

She took a deep breath and blocked everyone out until it was just Lucy and the elephants.

"Ja-Ja-John R-Robinson," she whispered.

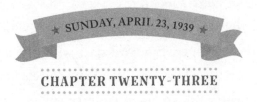
CHAPTER TWENTY-THREE

"YOU'RE ONE OF US."

Lucy felt stiff all over, like she'd just been thrashed with Mackinac's belt. But nothing happened. No one told her how stupid she was. And then she heard Grace's voice.

"Okay, Lucy, you're my elephant girl."

Grace's words filled Lucy's belly like hot chocolate on a cold day.

Nico bounced out of his shoes, pummeling her with affectionate punches. Eugene hugged her. Jabo handed her his handkerchief to wipe her cheeks.

Lucy could not stop smiling.

"Let's get you up on Jenny. You can ride her to the water wagon. I'll follow with Baby. We need to give them a good long drink before they board," Grace announced.

Lucy handed Eugene back his ace of hearts, her heart hammering with excitement.

"Leave your shoes here. It's easier to ride without them. Lots of ways to mount. But we'll start with this one." Grace tapped Jenny's shoulder. The elephant kneeled and Grace showed Lucy how to step up on Jenny's bent leg, grab hold of one waxy ear, and hoist herself up onto the elephant's broad back.

"Sit smack behind her ears and bend your legs. Keep them tucked," Grace instructed.

Lucy pulled her dress down and pushed her bottom forward. Her toes fit behind Jenny's ears. She liked the feeling of the elephant's wrinkly hide beneath her stocking feet.

"Place your hands on the top of her head," Grace called up to her.

Jenny's skin was tough but warm, with prickly hairs growing from it. The two globes at the top of her head were cushiony beneath the tough skin. Lucy liked having her palms there.

"Good. Now let's go."

Jenny lumbered forward after Grace, her enormous body moving on silent feet. It seemed impossible that such a big creature could make so little noise.

Lucy tried not to look down at the ground so far below. She focused on the top of Nico's head.

Lucy thought Grace looked like a princess when she rode, but now she realized it was the rhythm of the elephant's steps and the sway of her back that gave this impression. Lucy felt like a princess, too.

Jenny made her way back to the watering truck, stopping to explore a nearby tree. Lucy held on for dear life as Jenny strained up, hooking her trunk on a high branch. The elephant pulled hard, then—*crack!*—broke the branch off the tree.

"No," Grace said, but Jenny ignored her. She had worked hard for this branch and wasn't about to abandon it.

"No," Grace barked. Jenny stuffed another piece in her mouth, then lumbered on.

Lucy could not believe how much she loved riding Jenny. When they got to the next stand, she'd collect leftover fruits and vegetables from Nitty-Bitty for Jenny and Baby, and if there was a river, take the elephants to play. She would be the best elephant girl Grace had ever had.

When they got to the watering truck, Grace and Bunk were kidding each other. Nico looked up at Lucy. "That was amazing," he said as Jenny skimmed her trunk over the water.

It was amazing. Lucy Simone Sauvé riding an elephant! Then Lucy realized Nico was referring to her speaking.

That wasn't amazing. She sounded like an idiot. She hoped they would all forget it ever happened and she could go back to using her paper and pencil. Grace said she had to say two words. She'd said them, and now she was done.

Nico rattled on as Baby splashed water on them. "Hey, don't get me wet!" He jumped back.

Nico kept talking about what had happened. Lucy didn't

respond and he finally moved on to the topic of Bald Doris. "Guess who gave her an apprenticeship? Diavolo! He had to do his act with Jabo's dummy. Not much danger if you're throwing knives at a rag doll. No standing ovation like the one for Elephantoff. He was furious."

Lucy frowned. Having Diavolo jealous of Elephantoff couldn't be good. And having him throw knives at a spinning Doris? That was awful.

"Diavolo likes her hair. Yours wouldn't stay put."

Lucy took out her paper, and using her leg as a table she wrote, *Target girl is dangerous.*

She leaned down and handed the page to Nico.

Nico nodded. "Jabo said he'd talk to Diavolo about it. He doesn't think a kid should be a target girl, either."

On the way back to the elephant car, all the trucks and wagons that had been used to move equipment from Winter Quarters to the train yard were being driven up ramps and onto flatbed train cars. Most of the train doors were closed. Only the elephant car door was open, the steep steel ramp waiting.

Grace helped Lucy slip off, then she tied a rope around Jenny's neck and guided her up the train car ramp, her back barely clearing the door. Baby followed, heading for the apples, hay, grain, and potatoes inside.

"I give them goodies on the train. That way I don't have trouble loading. They're like my kids, those two. Especially

Baby," Grace explained as Lucy collected her shoes and followed Grace up the ramp.

When they were inside, the roustabouts stowed the ramp and shut the train car door *shunk-a-shunk-shunk,* leaving just enough room for a human to slip in and out.

There was another door on the short side and bars separating the two halves of the elephant car. On one side were the elephants. On the other was Lucy's bedroll, stacked in the corner with Nico's, Eugene's, and Doris's. Bunk must have had their stuff put there. He kept track of everything.

"The elephants are good on the train and they have plenty of food. We'll water them again when we get to Blue Creek. Okay, look . . . I'm giving you this chance, but I won't give you a second. Do you understand?"

Lucy nodded.

"Three rules, Lucy. One: Animals first. Before you eat, the elephants eat. Before you drink, the elephants drink. Your job is to make sure my animals are healthy and happy. Is that clear?

"Second: Go the extra mile. Jenny and Baby give their all every performance. I expect the same of you.

"Third: Don't lie, don't cheat, don't steal, don't sneak. I need to be able to trust you."

Grace dug out a pair of neatly folded blue farmer pants. "Bull hands wear coveralls," she explained, handing them to Lucy.

Lucy slipped on the coveralls. They felt strange. She had

never worn pants before. She kept her stockings and Betts's dress tucked underneath, which made her feel more like her normal self.

When she was ready to go, Grace looked up from the notebook. "One more thing . . . you can't expect an elephant to read your notes, Lucy. You'll have to talk to them."

Lucy swallowed hard.

"The OOFOs will be staying in the elephant car with you. I expect you to keep your eye on Doris. Baby is not fond of her."

The train whistle blew.

"Train's leaving in five minutes." Jabo clapped his hands as Doris, Nico, and Eugene climbed into the car, carrying supper boxes for all of them.

"Here are your meal tickets and your route card. Congratulations, honey." Grace shook her hand. "You're one of us."

Lucy couldn't take her eyes off the route card. Finally, it was hers.

PART THREE

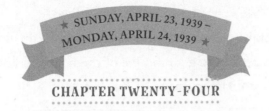

CHAPTER TWENTY-FOUR

"HE DOESN'T C-CARE...
ABOUT YOU."

Doris insisted they arrange the bedrolls so that Lucy was hidden. "Diavolo is still mad at you," Doris said.

"But she has an apprenticeship now," Nico said.

Doris shrugged. "So? He doesn't care."

Diavolo didn't like Lucy. But would he throw her off the train? Or was this just Doris causing trouble?

Red-lighting? Lucy wrote.

"He won't kick you off," Nico said.

"I dunno about that." Doris puffed her chest up.

The train moved forward, then backward, then forward again, as they hitched and unhitched cars, until finally the signalman's lantern flashed and they were on their way.

They had just finished eating when they heard the *ding-ding-ding* of a railway crossing and the hiss of train brakes.

191

Lucy stood up to peek out. Eugene joined her at the grimy window. "We're stopping already?" he asked.

The train pulled into a station, where a small group of passengers waited to get on. One of them looked familiar.

Lucy's stomach plunged. It was Frank!

"Hey, come see this!" Eugene motioned to Nico.

Nico peeked out the dirty window.

"He came," Nico said, stunned.

Doris crowded in next to them. "What's he doing here?"

"I told you I wired them," Nico mumbled.

"You said they weren't coming," Doris said.

"Changed his mind, I guess. Doesn't look like Alice is with him. Willy, either." A smile flickered across Nico's lips. "Guess Willy wasn't as smart as Frank thought."

"Willy was the little boy, right?" Doris asked.

Nico nodded.

Lucy took out her paper and started to write.

"Come on, Lucy. Just say it," Doris blurted out, yanking Lucy's pencil out of her hand.

Lucy glared at Doris. Doris would be the first to make fun of her if she stuttered.

Lucy's heart beat too fast. She stared at the elephants, opened her mouth, but her throat closed up so tightly she could hardly get the word out. "Wh-why?" she finally managed to whisper.

"To see me . . ." Nico's leg quivered.

"We went all the way to Chicago and he didn't want

192

anything to do with you," Doris said. "He gave me a dollar, but he didn't give you one cent."

Nico scowled at Doris; then he turned back to the sooty window. "I told him there was a poker game on the train," he whispered, barely audible.

"So? He could play poker anywhere," Doris said. "And why isn't Alice with him?"

Nico's eyes shifted. "Alice doesn't play poker," he mumbled, pushing open the door and stepping out onto the platform connecting the elephant car to the flat car in front.

Lucy followed him.

Nico turned when he saw her. "The game's in Diavolo's car. You can't come."

Lucy tried to make eye contact with Nico. "No!" he shouted. "I don't want you with me!"

Lucy grabbed his sleeve. He wheeled around. "Look, I owe him, okay? He got me off the streets. Nobody understands that."

Lucy's eyes didn't waver.

Nico looked away. "I'm just going to say hello," he muttered.

The train started up again. Lucy held on to the rail as they gathered speed, the cold air blowing her hair and whipping her clothes.

"I said go back!" Nico whispered.

"N-no," Lucy said.

"This is none of your business."

Lucy thought about the day Thomas Slater took her to

the orphanage. "Just until your mama gets back on her feet. She'll get better and we'll come get you," he had said. She had believed him. Of course she had.

Lucy didn't want to speak, but it was dark out here. He couldn't read the expressions on her face very well. She forced the words out. "How'd you . . . g-get to the orphanage?"

Nico squinted. "What are you talking about?"

"What did he say when he . . . l-left you?"

The side of Nico's face began to twitch. "I don't remember," he mumbled.

Lucy stared hard at him. He was lying.

Nico took a labored breath. "He said I'd be going to stay with his aunt for a little while."

The train roared on into the night, the moonlit meadows flying by. Their bodies rocked with the train's speed, and their arms bumped against each other, their cheeks rosy from the cold air.

"He doesn't c-care . . . about you. We do!"

"I was a beggar. I didn't have anything. He took me in. He gave me food. He taught me to read."

"And wh-when he didn't . . . need you?"

Nico turned away.

Lucy waited, watching him. But he didn't say a word and he didn't look her way. She waited for a long while; then she left him alone. Only he could decide.

To her surprise, Nico followed her.

The elephants were standing quietly. Eugene was asleep. Doris's eyes flickered open, then closed again. Lucy was so tired, she collapsed onto her bedroll, her head sinking into the pillow. She was almost asleep when Frank appeared.

His steps were unsteady in the speeding train.

"Nico, my man, thanks for the heads-up." Frank winked at Nico. Then he looked around. "They have you with the animals?" He shook his head. "You should come home, Nico."

Nico's lip twitched. He studied the straw bedding.

Frank's camel-hair coat was out of place in the elephant car. But he was so handsome. Who wouldn't want to be Frank's pretend son?

Nico got out of bed.

Frank put his arm around him. "You have no idea how much Alice and I have missed you, Nico."

Nico nodded.

Lucy stared at him. Nico would go with Frank. And when Frank and Alice grew tired of him, he'd be back at the orphanage again.

Lucy had lost him, and there was nothing she could do about it. But then a question floated through her sleepy mind and she sat up. "W-Willy?" she asked.

"Willy went to stay with my aunt for a little while," Frank said.

Nico stiffened.

A shadow crossed Frank's face. He'd made a mistake and he knew it. "Willy was only temporary. Not like you. You're part of the family, Nico," Frank said.

Nico's eyes were glassy. He stared at Lucy.

"Much as I'd like to continue talking to you, Lucy, I'm afraid Nico and I have to go. Game's about to start."

Nico didn't move.

Frank snapped his fingers in Nico's face. "Wake up, Nico."

Lucy held her hand out to Nico.

Nico took it.

Frank grinned. "I've taught you well. . . . You've got yourself a dame and everything. But don't forget what I told you about dames: there's always another one in the next town. Say goodbye to her, Nico." Frank's voice was smooth.

Nico tightened his grip on Lucy's hand. "No," he whispered.

Frank snorted. "Nico, I didn't take you for the sentimental type. Let's go!"

Nico's face hardened.

"Really, Nico? That's the thanks I get for all I've done for you?"

Nico looked away from Frank.

Frank sucked in his lips and shook his head. "You won't get another chance from me," he said, and then he walked out.

*   *   *

When he was gone, Nico woke Doris. "You know how to get into Diavolo and Seraphina's car?" he asked.

Doris nodded.

"Tell Diavolo to play with his own deck. Frank's cards are marked. Tell him if Frank drops his glasses under the table or starts coughing and needs water, watch out. Don't seat him next to a left-hander. And tell him I need Lucy's chances back in return for this information. And no matter what, don't let Frank see you."

"Got it," Bald Doris said, and hurried out.

In the morning when Grace slid the door open, the bright sun nearly blinded them. The roustabouts pulled out the ramp and they all climbed down.

"I did what you said." Doris ran her hand over the yellow peach fuzz on her head. "You owe me," she told Nico and Lucy.

"Th-thank you," Lucy said.

"Did you hear what I did?" Doris stuck her face in front of Eugene.

Eugene smiled at her. "Good job, Doris."

They all watched as Jenny cautiously made her way down the ramp, followed by Baby, who shot out, nearly falling on her face.

Grace and Lucy took the elephants to the watering truck, the unpacking in full swing. Bunk conducted the operation like a master puzzle maker. He knew what should come off first, which trucks should carry poles, and where to take the canvas rolls, stakes, and cook tent supplies. He knew where to find each performer's trunk and where each one should go.

The wind flattened Lucy's hair, blowing it in her face. Buckets bumped against the train. Feed bags flew by.

Rib and Nevada came to get Jenny. They slipped on her harness and took her to the other end of the train, where she would haul the tent poles to the circus site. Grace collected Baby, who was trumpeting for Jenny, startled by the banging buckets.

From the meadow came the sound of the roustabouts' hammers and chants. "Heave-ee, heave-ee, ho. Shake it, break it, let it go!"

By the time Jenny's hauling work was done, the cook tent and the menagerie tents were up. Lucy had Baby set up in the elephant corner of the menagerie tent with big stacks of hay, vegetables, and apples. She rubbed Jenny's legs with ointment and scratched her favorite spot. Then she washed her hands and headed for the cook tent, smiling to herself. Today was the first day she got to go to the cook tent with her very own breakfast ticket. She went the long way around the big top, which lay on the ground, the wind picking up corners and folding it over on itself.

She'd done just as Grace had asked. Grace had given her a rare smile. It was all working out, Lucy thought, and then she saw the old blue Ford parked outside.

Mackinac and Grundy!

Where were Doris, Nico, and Eugene? She had to warn them. Lucy took off running across the meadow.

But two of Diavolo's big roustabouts were running after her. They caught her by her coveralls.

Lucy tried to twist out of their grip. "B-Bunk! Bunk!" she shouted. But it was so windy, her words didn't carry.

Mackinac and Grundy stood by the car, clutching their hats to their heads and holding their dresses down.

Lucy shouted for help, but her words were lost in the wind.

Where was Jabo? Nico? Grace?

Lucy tried to twist out of the big men's hands, but one of them lifted her off the ground, slung her over his shoulder, and lumbered across the grass to the Ford.

"J-J-J-Jabo! J-Jabo! B-Bunk! Help! John R-R-Robinson John R-R-Robinson!" She beat her fists against his strong back.

"John—John . . . Robinson!"

Matron Mackinac opened the car door and the roustabout shoved Lucy inside. Lucy kicked and screamed, but the two big men leaned their weight against the door until Grundy could get behind the wheel and Mackinac could climb in the back. Mackinac grabbed Lucy and held her fast while Grundy drove down the rutty road.

Out the window the cook tent got smaller and smaller, and then it was gone.

March 11, 1939
Home for Friendless Children
Riverport, Iowa

Dear Lucy,

One moment I'm certain I will find you. The next
I'm sure it is lunacy to work all night for money to
travel to an orphanage, when you are not there. Every
day is like this, my hope going up and down like
the needle on my sewing machine. Every time I read
Mama's letter I get so excited I will find you. And then
I read Mrs. Mackinac's letters and down the needle
goes again. Where are you, Lucy? All I can think to do
is go see for myself.

Love,
Dilly

March 23, 1939
Home for Friendless Children
Riverport, Iowa

Dear Mrs. Mackinac,

Now you say that Lucy Sauvé "may have been" at your home but you are "not at liberty to say where she is now, as she has started a new life with the nice family who adopted her." You say seeing me would only "make the transition more difficult for her." You say it is "illegal" to tell me who has adopted her. This makes no sense to me, Mrs. Mackinac. Why would there be a law that prevents sisters from finding each other?

I understand that you can't let any person "off the street" look through your files. But I am not any person. I am the sister of a girl who was in your orphanage.

Yours truly,
Dilly Sauvé

P.S. One of the office girls got proposed to in a dress I made. All the girls want dresses now. I will have the $$ sooner than I was thinking before.

CHAPTER TWENTY-FIVE

ORPHAN ELEVEN

"This is the thanks we get?" Matron Mackinac hissed at Lucy as the old Ford rattled across the bridge.

Grundy glanced back at Mackinac and Lucy in the back seat. "Should've picked another one. Nothing but trouble from her."

"Wished that a hundred times if I wished it once," Mackinac said.

"What we've done for that child."

"Don't I know it. Never get any thanks, that's for sure," Mackinac grumbled.

Rage swelled inside Lucy. She dug her nails into the palms of her hands to keep herself in check.

"Gonna take her straight there," Grundy said.

Straight where? Reform school?

"What time are they expecting us?" Grundy asked.

"Nine-thirty," Mackinac said.

The car windows were fogged up. Grundy rolled her window down a crack. "Gonna be late."

Late where? Lucy wondered.

They were a long way from the circus, but still Lucy saw posters plastered in shop windows, on fences, and on telephone poles. Every time she spotted one, Lucy felt a warm hope flicker inside. But the longer they drove, the fewer she saw. Then they disappeared entirely.

Mackinac's grip on her arm had loosened. At the next red light, Lucy would pull open the door and dive out.

"Don't even think about it," Mackinac whispered, tightening her grasp.

Lucy shuddered. At the orphanage, the girls said Mackinac had a sixth sense. She knew what you were plotting almost before you did.

Mackinac smelled of cherry cough syrup and something sharp, like disinfectant. Lucy tried to scoot closer to the window, but the iron hand held her in place. Her arm hurt where Mackinac's fingers dug in.

Why hadn't Mackinac and Grundy looked for the other orphans? Why did Lucy matter to them, and not Doris, Nico, and Eugene? Mackinac couldn't stand Lucy. Why in the world would she want her back?

"We told them you had the flu. Are you listening to me, Lucy?" Mackinac demanded.

Lucy nodded. Mackinac's voice buzzed with importance when she said *them*. That usually meant she was talking about the university people.

"This is the position your nonsense has put us in," Mackinac said.

"Five hundred mouths to feed on a budget for two hundred and fifty. Fifty percent more than the orphanage was built for," Grundy agreed.

"How are we supposed to make that work?" Mackinac asked.

"We don't turn children away. Earned our place in heaven, that's for sure," Grundy said.

"But, Lucy, your selfishness has put everyone at risk," Mackinac scolded.

Lucy didn't see what she had to do with any of this. They should be happy to have one less mouth to feed.

"Now you listen to me." Matron Mackinac grabbed Lucy's chin and wrenched her head around until Lucy was looking straight at her. "You will cooperate fully."

Lucy nodded, trying to avoid Mackinac's piercing eyes.

"Your friends will not appreciate getting punished for your shenanigans. You chew on that for a while, young lady."

Lucy clenched her teeth, the rage rising inside.

At first, when Miss Holland told Matron Mackinac that Lucy hadn't been cooperative, Mackinac had thrashed Lucy with the superintendent's belt. She'd been given toilet scrubbing duty, and was made to sit in her chair while everyone ate supper. When Lucy still wouldn't open her mouth, Mackinac had punished Lucy's best friend Emma instead. That worked every time.

Now they rolled to a stop at a light, but she couldn't get away. Mackinac's fingers burned her arm. The light turned green again.

Lucy thought about Dilly and the route card. The first week in May, Saachi's would be in Chicago for a three-day stand. Today was April 24. Lucy had to catch up with the circus before Chicago. She'd never find Dilly locked away in that orphanage.

Lucy's elbow grazed the pocket of her dress underneath her coveralls. Inside the pocket were the precious route card, the silk purse with the elephant hairs, her baby tooth, her paper and pencil, and Dilly's button.

Would Jabo know what happened to her? Would Grace? Would they think she'd abandoned the elephants? She felt sick to her stomach thinking about it.

Grace trusted her. Bunk, Rib, and Jabo would back her up. They cared about her. She knew they did. She wasn't just an orphan anymore. She was an OOFO.

Mackinac and Grundy were arguing about which road to take. Mackinac prevailed, as always. A few minutes later they drove past large, stately buildings with foreign words on them. And then past more buildings with big pillars.

COLLEGE OF JOURNALISM one sign said. COLLEGE OF FINE ARTS read another. This was the university where rich people got to read as many books as they wanted.

How excited Lucy had been that day eighteen months ago when they told her she'd been chosen for a special honor: lessons from the university lady. Mackinac had said it was because Lucy was an A student, always the first to raise her hand in class. And because she had a beautiful voice. Lucy had made Mackinac proud.

Matron Grundy pulled into a parking space.

"Take off those ridiculous pants." Mackinac said. She had brought her a dress, but when she saw Lucy had the dress Betts had made for her underneath the coveralls, she didn't make her change.

The two flanked her as she walked up the steps to the building. Matron Grundy's wiry arm was linked through Lucy's. Matron Mackinac held her elbow with her iron grip.

They marched her into a hall and up the stairs, through a waiting room to a small office where Miss Holland sat with her stinging smile.

When Lucy had first met Miss Holland, she dreamed Miss Holland would adopt her and sew her dresses the way Mama had. She imagined Miss Holland bringing her great stacks of books and sheet music to help her sing solos. But Miss Holland didn't ask Lucy to sing, and she didn't care what Lucy thought.

At first, Lucy had thought Miss Holland beautiful, with her dark wavy hair and blue eyes. But now it was painful to look at her. It was Miss Holland's scorn that had made Lucy hate her own mouth. Hate her own stupid tongue.

"We've missed you, Lucy," Miss Holland said with a chilly smile. "So glad you're feeling better now."

Lucy studied her shoes. She imagined the feel of Baby's trunk. The way her big flat feet liked to splash. She thought of Jenny's lumbering walk. The coarse feel of her hair.

Miss Holland turned to Mackinac. "Take about an hour," she said.

Matron Mackinac leaned down and whispered in Lucy's ear, "Do exactly what she says. Do you hear me?"

When Miss Holland had come to the orphanage, the sessions were held late in the afternoon in Matron Grundy's small office. They were never at the university.

Why was she here?

The room had sunny bright windows, leather armchairs, and framed degrees on the walls. On a shelf were slates, notepads, machines with long paper readouts, and machines that measured hand strength. Lucy remembered when Miss Holland had brought the machines to the orphanage.

"So, Lucy, Dr. Smithson will be joining us to observe. I'll let him know you're here." She hustled out.

Lucy tracked her to the door, but when it opened, she saw Mackinac and Grundy seated like guards in the next room.

Miss Holland pulled the door closed, preventing Mackinac's and Grundy's prying eyes from seeing. When the latch clicked, Lucy flew to the window. The office was on the fourth floor, but there was no balcony and the window didn't open.

What if there was a fire? Could Lucy shout the word "fire"? Could she get by Mackinac and Grundy?

Then she noticed the file sitting on a table. ORPHAN ELEVEN, GROUP B, FLUENCY STUDY the tab read.

Lucy flipped open the file and read the handwritten notes inside.

Age nine at the onset of the study. She has no known living relations.

Orphan Eleven is intelligent, with strong verbal skills. She possesses above-average speech and fluency. No marked hesitancy. Orphanage personnel chose her for this study because she is an enthusiastic student. "Eager to please," they said.

Rebecca Holland has seen Orphan Eleven for fifty-five minutes, once a week, since the study onset in October 1937. Miss Holland has worked with the orphanage personnel to continue the training in all interactions with Orphan Eleven. Orphanage personnel were cooperative with all aspects of the study.

The children in Group B, the fluent-speaker group, were told they had begun to stutter and needed to correct this problem immediately or it would grow much worse. Assistants worked with them to create consistent doubt about their speaking abilities.

They were told that if they didn't stop stuttering, their prospects in life would be bleak.

Orphan Eleven's progress is proving Dr. Smithson's thesis: Stuttering is a learned behavior. A parent's constant criticism can cause it.

Since shortly after the onset of the study, Orphan Eleven has demonstrated a desperate fear of opening her mouth. Every week she becomes more withdrawn. When coerced to speak, she demonstrates typical stutterer behavior, such as gasping and leaving long silences between words

Lucy heard the outer door opening and footsteps approaching. She slammed the file closed and dashed back to the chair. The door opened and a gray-haired man in a white lab coat and dark-rimmed spectacles came in, followed by Miss Holland. Miss Holland sat in a chair across from Lucy. The gray-haired man sat at the desk.

"Let's start at the beginning, shall we?" Miss Holland suggested. "What is your name?"

Lucy stared at Miss Holland. Her stomach hurt, her head felt light. Then she saw the gray-haired man pick up the file and begin making notes.

"Lucy, your name," Miss Holland barked.

Now everything made sense. She was valuable to them because she had proved Dr. Smithson's theory correct. The criticism and constant humiliation had been intentional. They had done it to make her stutter.

Lucy closed her mouth so tightly it made her jaw ache.

She sat up straight, drilling her feet into the floor. The one thing she absolutely would not do was stutter.

But she'd been trying not to stutter since her sessions with Miss Holland had begun. The only way to keep from being shamed was to keep her mouth shut.

Then, in the whirl of thoughts, Bald Doris popped into her mind. Doris had caught her singing in the bathroom once. Lucy didn't stutter when she sang.

Lucy stared defiantly at Miss Holland, imagining a tune for her name. Then she opened her mouth, and in her clear soprano she sang, "Sauvé. Sauvé. My name is Lucy Simone Sauvé."

Miss Holland's eyes narrowed. "That is not what I asked for."

Lucy shrugged, but she couldn't keep the smile off her face.

"Say your name. *Say it.* Don't sing it. Dr. Smithson is observing. Don't waste his time."

Lucy stared at the man in the lab coat.

No. No. No.

"Lucy, your name!" Miss Holland barked.

Lucy hated Miss Holland's criticizing voice. Hated how it had gotten inside her head. How she couldn't open her mouth without hearing Miss Holland and Matron Mackinac's ridicule.

"This will be a lifelong problem. No man will marry you. No boss will hire you. You will not be able to make your way in the world, unless you let us help you."

Lucy had believed them. Until now.

Lucy shook her head, her ponytail brushing across her face. "N-no," she whispered.

"See how she's struggling." Miss Holland's eyes drifted to the man in the lab coat. He nodded his approval. Miss Holland gave him a small, triumphant smile.

"We can help you. That's why we're here," Miss Holland said in her smooth lying voice. "Please repeat my words exactly as I say them: My name is Lucy Sauvé."

Lucy considered the word "help" as if it were on her vocabulary list. Help meant making something easier for someone. But when Miss Holland said the word "help," it meant something else entirely.

Lucy sat in stony silence while the man in the lab coat made notes in the file. Her file. The one that said *Orphan Eleven.*

"If you waste our time here, we'll need to inform Matron Mackinac. We would prefer not to do that, but . . ." Miss Holland let her sentence trail off.

"She is st-stubborn," the man in the lab coat said.

Lucy stared at him. His name, Dr. Smithson, that was the name in the file. He had designed the study and he stuttered.

None of this made sense.

Lucy began to write, but Miss Holland yanked her paper away.

Lucy glared at her. She had never hated anyone this much.

"One thing . . . I . . . know"—Lucy took a big gulping breath—"y-you are . . . not t-trying to help me."

"She can't get a sentence out without pauses and repetition." Miss Holland beamed at the man, ignoring the content of Lucy's words as she always did.

"Good work, M-Miss Holland." He nodded.

Good work?

Lucy grabbed her paper back and wrote, *I spoke fine before I started working with you.* Her hand shook as she shoved the page in Miss Holland's face.

"She writes her responses. A key trait of selective mutism," Miss Holland reported to Dr. Smithson.

"I c-can see that." He nodded, his eyes bright, the corner of his mouth twitching as if he was trying hard not to smile.

Lucy could not stop staring at him. The horror of her time with Miss Holland was a victory for him!

Lucy's voice busted out of her, unstoppable. "You . . . cannot do this to me! I am not . . . your Orphan Eleven."

March 24, 1939

Dear Lucy,

I'm getting up every morning at three and going to Mrs. LaFinestre's. Mrs. LaFinestre gave me a key and she leaves the light on for me. She lets me use machine #71 so long as I don't sew my dresses during work time. I sell my dresses to the office girls. They are happy because I make them look pretty.

Sometimes it seems like all the girls have family around them and dates and parties they need dresses for. And then there is me, one lone girl sewing. Maybe you are gone & I will never find you. But I'm not giving up. Even if I go to Riverport and do not find one single thing about where you went to, I will have tried with my whole self to put together what Thomas Slater broke apart.

Love,
Dilly

April 13, 1939
Home for Friendless Children
Riverport, Iowa

Dear Mrs. Mackinac,

I have not heard anything back from my last letter.
I will be in Riverport on April 24. Please could you
send me directions of how to get to your orphanage
from the train station? I need them right away.

Yours truly,
Dilly Sauvé

April 14, 1939

Dear Lucy,

Remember how we would tell Mrs. Three Eyes things we didn't want to say to each other? I wish I had Mrs. Three Eyes now, because there is one thing I haven't told you.

It isn't as bad as Thomas Slater telling Mama he was rich and had a car and a home when he had nothing, but it's awful bad just the same.

My plan was to write it here. But I can't. I don't want to see the words in black-and-white on this page. Maybe you could hear my sorry without knowing all I did.

Love,
Dilly

P.S. The last time I saw Mrs. Three Eyes she was packed in Mama's suitcase. I hope she's with you.

CHAPTER TWENTY-SIX

OOFOS LOOKED OUT FOR EACH OTHER.

O n the way out, Lucy heard Dr. Smithson talking to a man with a beard that fanned out from his chin like a skirt. "Nice when the results support your hypothesis this way," the bearded man said.

Dr. Smithson smiled. He stood up straighter. His eyes shone.

He was proud of what he'd done.

Why would the orphanage have allowed her to be a part of this terrible study?

The question went around in Lucy's mind as the car's ignition turned over without catching. Did they think the study would help the orphans? That was what Matron Mackinac had said when she explained the program to Lucy. But Mackinac had to see that the sessions were designed to create problems.

216

She had to have realized what the time with Miss Holland was doing to Lucy.

Mackinac had to know the truth. She had to.

The Ford's ignition turned over *ur-urr urrr,* then finally caught, and Grundy backed out of the parking space.

Lucy stared out the window at the university buildings. Then she thought about the shiny new orphanage oven, the thick wool orphan coats, the boxes of chocolates and caramels for the matrons. Had the university given the orphanage gifts in exchange for using Lucy for their study?

That was why Mackinac and Grundy wanted her and not Doris, Nico, and Eugene. Lucy was valuable to them because she was in the study.

Lucy stared out at the houses, the white church steeple, the sign welcoming them to Riverport. The car had slowed and Mackinac's grip on Lucy's arm had loosened. Lucy could yank free and dive out. But once again, Mackinac sensed Lucy's thoughts and tightened her grip.

Soon, the wrought-iron fence and the sad gray cottages of the orphanage came into view. How familiar and how different they looked.

The fence was tall, but it was just a fence. It made her ashamed of the power she'd let it have over her. She wouldn't let their fence stop her again.

The old car bumped up the road to its parking spot by the incinerator. Mackinac was scolding, "It is only out of the goodness of our hearts that we didn't take you straight to reform school. But if you give us any more trouble . . . if you get called out and sent to the chairs *even once*"—spit flew out of her mouth—"we will deliver you that very day. Do you understand?"

The reform school in Elman was a few hours' drive from the orphanage. Miss Holland wouldn't want to drive all the way to Elman every week. It was an empty threat. They weren't going to send her to Elman at all.

Lucy longed to tell Mackinac that. She wanted to see the reaction on her face when Mackinac understood that Lucy had figured out exactly what was going on. But she knew it would only make Mackinac angrier, which would mean more restrictions. It was better to play along.

"And not a word about where you've been," Mackinac said.

Lucy nodded, her eyes on her lap.

They walked by the schoolroom window, where girls sat at old wooden desks huddled over their lesson books. Mackinac pushed open the door and heads popped up. Everyone stared at Lucy as she walked down the aisle between the desks.

They were gaping at the dress Betts had made for her and the shoes she'd gotten from Diavolo. Girls who came back from running away were dirty, torn, and tattered in their ill-fitting orphanage dresses. No girl had ever run away and come back looking better than when she left.

Lucy stopped at her old seat, the one reserved for the top student, but nine-year-old Ruby with the golden brown skin and eyes that made a person want to keep looking at her was sitting in it. Lucy grinned at Ruby.

"In the back," Mackinac barked, conferring with the teacher, Matron Johnston.

As soon as Lucy settled into her seat, the notes began flying. *How did you get that dress? What did you eat? What happened to Bald Doris? Were there boys with you?*

Lucy slipped the notes into her pocket. She knew better than to answer them with Mackinac and Johnston there. She opened the math book and began to read.

When the bell rang and they were excused to the dining hall, the girls swarmed Lucy. Everyone wanted to sit next to her.

The midday meal was broth that smelled vaguely of lamb and was the color of worn underwear, and a crust of bread. Hungry as Lucy was, she gave her food to Ruby, who sat by her.

"Try it. We got a new cook, remember? The food isn't so bad anymore," Ruby said.

Lucy looked out at the faces waiting to hear what had happened to her and wished for Emma. How nice it would be to tell Emma about Saachi's!

But the other girls might make fun of her. It wasn't like talking to Nico and Eugene. Besides, Mackinac said not to talk about where she'd been.

Still, these girls needed to know what the world was like

outside the fence. They were OOFOs, even if they didn't know what that was yet. OOFOs looked out for each other. And anyway, Mackinac and Grundy were in the matrons' dining room.

Lucy took a deep breath and forced the words out. "I was . . . at the c-circus."

"You're talking!" a girl said.

"Like you used to," another said.

"Yay!" a few girls cheered.

Lucy nodded and kept on. "S-Saachi's circus is the . . . most wonderful . . . ," she began. But the more she talked, the more doubt she saw in their eyes.

They didn't believe her.

It was only when she described the food that their eyes grew wide. The round meatballs you cut with a fork. The peanut butter cookies. The stack of pancakes with butter melting on the top.

After lunch Mackinac appeared and Lucy went quiet. But a girl who had been a friend of Doris's ran straight to Mackinac and told her everything Lucy had said.

Mackinac's face grew red and her eyes bulged. She swooped down on the girls. "Chores! Now!" she barked, and the girls scurried off to their chore areas.

Then Mackinac dragged Lucy out of the dining hall. "You come with me," she said.

April 16, 1939
R&M Dresses
Chicago, Illinois

Dear Mrs. LaFinestre,

I know you don't like when we girls talk about personal business. But I don't think you'll hold my job unless you understand how important it is for me to take off two days to go to Riverport. The days are April 24 & 25.

I'm going to find my little sister. She is the only family I have left. I'm going to search an orphanage for her, because my mama said that's where she was.

I understand if you have to let another girl use machine #71 while I'm gone. But please could I have it when I get back? This is a lot to ask, but you won't be sorry. When I get home, you will say no girl ever worked so hard for you as Dilly Sauvé.

Yours truly,

Dilly Sauvé

April 24, 1939

Dear Lucy,

I'm so excited I could not even swallow one spoonful of oatmeal this morning. Today I am going to the orphanage where Mama said you were. I'm hoping to talk to Mrs. Mackinac. I'm hoping she will see me. Maybe then I'll find out where you went. Maybe I will meet someone who knew you. Maybe you told one of the girls about me. I only have two days in Riverport. I hope that will be enough.

The thought of going there has made me feel like there is a moth caught in my chest and it is flying all around trying to get out. I wonder if you miss me the way I miss you.

Love,
Dilly

CHAPTER TWENTY-SEVEN

A TEAKETTLE WHISTLING

Mackinac towed Lucy across the grass to the matrons' cottage. Running from here would be easier. The back door of the small house was outside the fence.

Then Lucy remembered the rumors about the attic room. Girls were locked in there. And left for days.

A shiver traveled down her spine.

But inside the cottage it was warm and cozy, with crocheted blankets on the chairs, pictures on the walls, and a teakettle whistling on the stove. It was a real house.

Mackinac pushed Lucy up the stairs and down a hall to a second stairwell steeper than the first.

The stairwell ceiling was low, the walls dark. Dust rose from each stair. Lucy sneezed. Mackinac prodded her from behind. "Didn't I tell you not to run your mouth about where you'd been?" she asked.

At the landing, Mackinac shoved Lucy into the attic room, which was barely bigger than Baby and just tall enough for Lucy to stand. Cobwebs floated off the walls. Dead flies and mousetraps were scattered across the floor. A greasy film clung to the dormer window.

"We want our girls to become pillars of society. Not the kind of drifters and outcasts the circus attracts."

Lucy's teeth cut into her tongue. She stared down at her shoes, trying to keep the explosion of anger in her chest from showing on her face.

"I won't have you ruining our girls."

Lucy nodded.

"You do know what happens to girls who run a second time. . . ."

Of course she knew. They shaved your head and put you on the reform-school list. But like reform school, the lice cut was an empty threat. Mackinac wouldn't want to explain a bald head to Miss Holland.

"You're to stay here until you've had a change of heart."

"I've had a ch-change of heart." Lucy nodded, doing her best to look apologetic. "I—I . . . have—"

But Mackinac didn't listen. She pulled the warped door closed and turned the key.

Lucy waited until Mackinac's footsteps had receded. Then she tried the knob. The lock rattled, but the door didn't budge.

No matter what she did, she couldn't get away from Mackinac and Miss Holland.

You brought this on yourself, the mean voice in her head said.

"Shut up!" Lucy shouted, kicking the door. "Shut up, shut up, sh-shut up!"

She looked around at the attic. Wooden crates were stacked on one side. A dusty pair of crutches was strewn across the floor. Lucy kicked a mousetrap out of the way and banged on the window.

Mackinac was gone. She had an orphanage to run. But there had been a teakettle whistling. Someone else was here.

They wouldn't help her.

No matron wanted trouble with Mackinac.

Maybe Lucy could get a note to one of the girls. She could break the window with a crutch, find something to weight the note, and toss it down. But it would land outside the fence, where no orphans were allowed to go. And even if an orphan got the message, it was doubtful she'd help Lucy.

Orphans didn't want trouble with Mackinac, either.

Maybe she could escape when they came to give her supper. She would pounce when the door opened, then run like the dickens. But would they even bother to bring her a meal?

What about water?

Lucy grew thirsty wondering about this.

She could try to pick the lock, but she had no hairpins.

She pulled the crates closer to see what was inside. One

was full of old newspapers yellowed with age. Another held fabric scraps, a doll with no head, and a needle and thread.

Lucy stuck the needle in the lock, moving it east, west, north, and south. When she connected with what she thought might be the locking lever, she pushed the needle deeper, but the lock didn't open. She pushed harder and the needle snapped in two.

Lucy kicked the door. She'd almost had it.

One needle wasn't strong enough. But maybe two. She found the two halves and put them together, but when she stuck them in the lock, they were too short to grip.

She went back to the box, took out all the fabric scraps, and shook each one. Then she ran her fingers along the bottom.

No more needles.

Lucy stood at the dormer window imagining what might be happening at Saachi's. First they would be performing and then packing and loading the train. Eugene setting up box suppers, Nico hanging up his ringmaster clothes, Bald Doris filling Diavolo's glass with ice water. But who would be helping with the elephants?

Back and forth Lucy paced the small room. Three steps one way. Three steps the other. She was hungry and she had a hammering headache. The attic smelled weird, like dust, medicine, and old shoes. She pushed the dead flies into a corner, made a pillow from fabric scraps, and curled up on the floor, holding Dilly's button in one hand and the silk pouch with the elephant hairs in the other.

When she woke, it was dark and she was angry at herself for sleeping so long.

She emptied her pockets and set all her belongings on her skirt: one pencil, one folded-up paper, Dilly's button, the silk pouch with the elephant hairs, the route card, and the baby tooth. She pulled the tail hairs out of the pouch and wound them around her fingers. She didn't know if they were from Baby or Jenny. Why had she never thought to ask?

She opened her paper. On the front was part of the circus poster with dancing horses. Then she studied the route card with the picture of Diavolo and Seraphina and the dates and cities of every stand. When she knew them by heart, she slipped everything back in her pockets and jumped up with new energy. She would find a way out.

Her eyes lit upon the crutches and she thought about how Nico had convinced the crowd Baby wasn't a terrified elephant stampeding from the big top but a pachyderm with a headache heading to the pharmacy for aspirin. What if Lucy banged on the door and when the matron came, Lucy said Mackinac had sent her up here to get the crutches?

Lucy didn't think anyone would believe that the attic door had locked by accident. But an elephant wouldn't go to a pharmacy, either. Nico had made the audience believe.

Lucy closed her eyes and imagined an emergency where a girl needed crutches. Then she banged on the door.

Nobody came.

She opened her hands and slapped the door. Then closed her fists and beat on it. "Ex-excuse me. I n-need help!"

Still nobody.

"H-help! Help!" she hollered. She was surprised at how easy it was to shout. Maybe because there was no one to hear.

Her fists grew sore, but she kept pounding and shouting.

At last, she heard slow steps on the stairs, then fumbling hands unlocking the door. A lady with a white apron and a sweet round face stood in the doorway, a box of baking soda in her hands. The cook!

Lucy took a deep breath. "There was an accident in cottage three. Margaret sprained her ankle. M-Mackinac said to run up and g-get the crutches for her."

The cook furrowed her brow. "Say what?"

"Mackinac said bring the crutches. Run as f-fast as I can. Margaret's too heavy to be carried."

Lucy held her breath.

The cook frowned. "But why are you—"

"I h-have to go." Lucy slipped past the cook and darted down the stairs, holding the crutches. She flew down the hall and headed for the next set of stairs, the cook's feet pounding behind her.

"Wait!" the cook called.

Then Mackinac's voice filled the entryway.

Lucy dove into the hall closet, falling back against the dresses as she maneuvered the crutches inside.

No sooner did she get the door closed then it opened again. Mackinac!

But it wasn't Mackinac. It was the cook.

"Go back," the cook whispered, panting, "and I'll help you."

Emma had liked the cook. The cook had given Emma handfuls of sugar. She'd spoken highly of Emma to another family she worked for and Emma had been adopted.

But Lucy didn't know if the cook could be trusted. Still, what choice did she have? If she refused, the cook would tell Mackinac she was hiding in the closet.

Lucy ran back up to the attic, shut the door behind her, and waited. Voices echoed in the hall, then footsteps on the stairs. The key rattled in the lock.

The door wasn't locked. Lucy couldn't lock it from the inside. Would Mackinac notice?

When the door opened, it was the cook who held the key. Mackinac loomed behind her.

"So," Mackinac said. "What do you have to say for yourself?"

Lucy took a deep breath. "I'm s-sorry. It was a . . . a mistake to run away. It won't happen again. It was . . . awful out there." She tried her best to cry.

Mackinac narrowed her eyes.

"Like I said, I heard her crying up here. Poor little thing. She learned her lesson. Oh yes she did," the cook said.

Mackinac glanced at her watch, then turned to the cook. "You're here awfully late."

"Ran out of baking soda. Knew you had some here. Had to get my dough ready. Got to be refrigerated overnight."

Mackinac's eyes lit up. "Chocolate crinkle cookies?"

"Oh yes, ma'am," the cook said.

Mackinac smiled, then considered Lucy. "Well, I suppose I can't leave you in here much longer," she muttered. "Come along. But not a word about that silly circus, do you understand?"

Lucy nodded. But all she could think about was the cook. The cook had helped her, just like she'd said she would.

CHAPTER TWENTY-EIGHT

THE BLUE FORD

Lucy guessed it was eight or eight-thirty when Mackinac walked her across the grass to cottage three. She wondered if she would have the same cot in the same spot by the radiator. Her pillow and her blanket would be orphan-borrowed. She'd be stuck with the old blanket, moth-eaten and smelling of urine. And she'd have to sleep without a pillow.

It was strange how familiar this place was and yet it felt like years since she'd lived here. But Mackinac didn't take her to the dorm room; she took her to the chairs. Lucy found her seat, second row, third from the left, and sat down. She folded her hands in her lap and placed her feet flat on the floor.

Being sent to the chairs was a punishment she didn't mind

that much. The night matron brooked no nonsense, but she left you alone if you were quiet. The chairs felt familiar, almost comfortable, and it gave her time to plan.

Running at night would be challenging. The night matron sat in the dorm room until all the girls were asleep. Then she walked down the hall to her room. Lucy would have to get by her, avoid the trip cord on the stairs that rang the bell, then get past the matron on the lower floor, who never seemed to sleep at all. Once outside, she'd need to climb the twelve-foot-tall fence somehow. But its vertical wrought-iron bars had ornaments and spikes, painful to grip. Last year a boy had fallen off it. Another time, a girl had been found on the orphanage side, frostbitten so badly she'd lost two fingers.

That was winter, though. It was nearly May now. Even so, Lucy did not know how she'd get over the fence.

Maybe she should run during chores. Afternoon chore time was longer than morning chore time, and the matrons were used to orphans being out and about raking leaves, cleaning chicken coops, digging holes to plant bushes, hauling laundry and trash.

Even so, she'd still have to get over the fence. And in broad daylight, too.

Then she thought of the blue Ford parked next to the incinerator. Grundy drove it to town every morning. Maybe Lucy could hide under a blanket in the back.

*   *   *

It was close to eleven by the time the night matron set down her knitting and walked Lucy back to the dorm room. Lucy didn't change out of the dress Betts had made, knowing it would be orphan-borrowed if she did. She climbed onto her squeaky old cot and pulled up the blanket that smelled of other people's misery.

The night matron settled in, a shawl on her lap, a book in her hand, and a small bag of candies in her pocket. Lucy pretended to sleep. But the matron stayed on and on, popping candies in her mouth and moving her lips as she read.

Lucy rolled over and stared out the window at the big yellow moon. Saachi's would be loaded on the train, headed for Little Junction now. She wiggled the route card out of her pocket and held it under the blanket until she heard the matron stand up and make her way down the hall, tapping her cane as she went. Lucy tipped the card toward the moonlight so she could read the list of dates and cities. She knew them by heart, but she liked to see them anyway. The card made it feel like the last nine days had been real.

In the morning, no girls asked questions. None wrote notes. None looked her way, all eyes on the matron.

"We got in trouble for talking to you," Ruby whispered when the matron stepped out of the room.

Lucy nodded. Just as well. It would be easier to get away if the girls weren't paying close attention to her.

Lucy went over her plan in her head as she and Ruby walked side by side to breakfast. The best time to duck out would be when the girls were walking down to the school building. She finished her bowl of gruel, which tasted better than usual—the food had improved slightly since the new cook had been hired. She put her dirty dish in the bin and stole out the door.

"Where you going in such a hurry?" the matron with the cane asked.

Stomach problems, Lucy wrote.

The matron nodded. "All right," she said.

In the bathroom, Lucy waited until the matron had moved on. Then she picked up the trash bucket, ducked back out the door, and walked fast to the incinerator.

If anyone stopped her, she would say a matron had asked her to empty the trash. But no one did. In the distance, boys were walking down to the school building, busy trying to trip each other.

She dropped the trash bucket by the incinerator and circled the blue Ford, her eyes scanning the surrounding area.

Her hands shook when she tested the door. Locked. The windows rolled up.

She tried the other side. Also locked. Then her hand found the trunk handle, which stuck at first, then popped open. Lucy took a quick look around and hopped inside.

But once she lay crouched in the dark trunk, her pulse quickened. She'd planned to hold the door down from the inside so that it looked shut. But what if the car went over a bump and the trunk closed? There was no lever to open the trunk from the inside. How would she get out?

Then she heard footsteps. The driver's-side door opened and the car shook as someone climbed in.

The door slammed shut. The motor turned over. *Urr, urr, urrr, urrr. Urr, urr, urrr, urrr.* Lucy bunched up the hem of her skirt and stuck it between the trunk lid and the car to keep it from closing.

Grundy turned the motor off. Waited a minute, then tried again.

Urr, urr, urrr, urrr.

"Come on," Grundy mumbled.

The minutes ticked by.

Urr, urr, urrr, urrr. Urr, urr, urrr, urrr.

"Darn thing," Grundy said.

The car shook as Grundy got out. Then the door slammed shut and Grundy walked away.

Now what? If Lucy wasn't in class, Mackinac would be called and the matrons would search the grounds.

Lucy hopped out of the trunk and ran all the way to the school building, then slipped into her seat just as Mrs. Johnston was putting her roll book away.

Mrs. Johnston waggled her eyebrows at Lucy.

Stomach problems. Lucy showed the paper where she had written this before.

Mrs. Johnston nodded. "Ruby said you weren't feeling well."

Lucy nodded, trying to hide her surprise. Ruby had covered for her. It was rare to find a girl who would go out of her way for you at the Home for Friendless Children.

CHAPTER TWENTY-NINE

LUCY SIMONE SAUVÉ

All during class Lucy thought about what to do. The blue Ford idea had worked well, if only the car had started. Should she try again tomorrow? Lucy didn't want to wait that long. Besides, the trunk was too risky. She knew that now.

By the time she'd finished lunch, Lucy had a lot of ideas about how to escape, but none of them seemed quite right. She stood in line waiting to receive her afternoon chore assignment, mulling them over. Most orphans got different chores every day, but since the bad reports from Miss Holland had begun, Lucy had been assigned scrubbing toilets and cleaning the bathrooms every afternoon. Maybe she could say the toilets overflowed. There weren't a lot of toilets at the orphanage, and the ones they had didn't work properly. That would give her a reason to run to the office, but then what?

Mackinac stood at the door holding the chore chart as she always did, but today the cook appeared, her apron crisp and clean. She whispered to Mackinac and Mackinac nodded.

When it was Lucy's turn in line, Mackinac said, "Kitchen. Wait here. I'll walk you over."

What? Lucy's mouth fell open.

Kitchen wasn't a punishment. It was the best chore assignment there was. Kitchen crew meant extra food.

"I'm in the kitchen too," Ruby said, standing with Lucy.

Lucy nodded, trying to understand how this had happened. The cook had said she'd help Lucy, but she'd done that already. She'd pretended to unlock the door and then she'd convinced Mackinac that Lucy had spent enough time in the attic.

Mackinac walked with Lucy and Ruby. She didn't lecture. Or hold Lucy by the arm. They were behind the fence now. She was confident nothing would happen.

When they got to the kitchen, the cook was wiping down the counters.

"Keep an eye on her and make her work," Mackinac said.

"Yes indeedy." The cook nodded, handing Ruby and Lucy white aprons, which they slipped over their dresses.

Ruby got a bucket and turned on the hot water spigot. When the bucket was full, Lucy helped her carry it to the pantry. Ruby picked up a scrub brush and handed Lucy a mop.

Lucy was busy mopping when Mackinac walked out. A minute later, the cook appeared. "Last night I couldn't sleep.

Got to thinking . . . putting two and two together. Tell me your full name, child."

Lucy stared at her. Why did she want to know?

"It's okay, honey. Just tell me." There was genuine concern in the cook's eyes.

Lucy Simone Sauvé, Lucy wrote.

"Sauvé?"

Lucy nodded.

"What's your sister's name?"

"D-Dilly."

"Oh, child," the cook whispered, crossing herself. "Your Dilly was here just yesterday!"

A choke caught in Lucy's throat. She tried to shake her head but was too stunned to move.

It was a lie.

Everything in this place was a lie. Don't trust anyone.

The cook raised her fuzzy eyebrows. "Oh yes, she was. Looks like you, except all growed up. Same red hair and freckles. She was in Mackinac's office. Mackinac had me pour tea and serve toast and jam. The matron's food, of course.

"She wanted to search the place, your Dilly did. But they told her you was dead, child. Then they dug out a doll they had in your file. Funny little thing with curled-up hair and an extra eye"—she touched the bridge of her nose—"right here."

Lucy gasped. Mrs. Three Eyes!

Mackinac had said personal toys and keepsakes only

caused trouble with the girls. She'd told Lucy it was for the best that someone had stolen Mrs. Three Eyes. It hadn't occurred to Lucy that that someone was Mackinac.

"The look on your Dilly's face when she saw that doll near broke my heart. She been missing you for an awful long while. Saw that clear as day."

"Where is . . . D-Dilly now?" Lucy whispered, gripping the button in her pocket.

"Heading back on the train, I expect. Said she was leaving today. I thought it was strange them locking you up. That Mackinac got a mean streak."

"Are y-you sure?" Lucy asked.

"I don't know if she's still here, child. She didn't say what time she'd be leaving."

"Maybe you can catch her," Ruby whispered.

The cook took a deep breath, her big chest rising and falling. "Don't know how you gonna do that. But you two are smart cookies. First desk, aren't you both?"

They nodded.

"You figure out something. I will help any way I can. Just don't get me fired. I got a house full of mouths to feed, all right?"

Lucy nodded, but all she could think was Dilly had come.

★ TUESDAY, APRIL 25, 1939 ★

CHAPTER THIRTY

THE ROUTE CARD

"**G**et busy with those mops. Mackinac sticks her head in here, we got to look like we're working. If you keep your voices low, I won't be able to make out one word you say." The cook winked at them.

Ruby sloshed her brush in the water. "How about if we dig a hole under the fence."

"S-someone would see us digging." Lucy stared at the clock. If she was to catch Dilly, every moment counted. "If we h-had a big . . . box. The cook could g-give me to the mailman."

"Don't think we have a box that big," Ruby said.

Slat-sided crates were stacked by the door, but they were small. "Maybe when the delivery . . . men come," Lucy suggested.

Ruby raced over to the cook, who was slicing onions, her eyes watering.

The cook shook her head. "Deliveries are Mondays and Thursdays." She rubbed her eyes on her sleeve. "I could say I was sending the flour back. Weevils. It's happened before. Ruby, climb up and get the flour bags."

Ruby stepped on a crate and pulled folded flour bags down from the pantry shelf, but they were too small to fit inside.

"I c-could sew them together," Lucy said.

Lucy could baste them together to make a bigger bag. But the sewing room was a five-minute run from here. And she would have to come up with a reason why she needed a needle and thread. Then she'd need time to sew the bags together.

"You don't have much time to catch your sister. She could be getting on that train this very minute," the cook said.

Lucy watched her transfer onions from the cutting board to the pan. "Deliveries . . . come in. What g-goes out?"

Ruby stared up at the ceiling, thinking. "Empty crates, empty flour bags, rags, and kitchen towels that need washing."

"Laundry!"

"Goes to the laundry room."

Lucy nodded. "There's always . . . t-too much."

Mounds of dirty clothes, pee-soaked sheets, threadbare towels, sweaty undershirts. It all piled up outside the laundry. The girls had to boil the clothes, then scrub, wring, and hang them. Backbreaking work in the steamy laundry room.

"What if . . . the cook needed her . . . her . . . towels

washed right away? What if she had to w-wash them . . . at home?" Lucy asked.

"The laundry bin!" Ruby said.

By the back door was a large canvas bag set in a metal frame with wheels. If Lucy rolled herself into a ball, she could fit inside and they could load the dirty towels and aprons on top of her.

The cook massaged her chin. "Oh, they'll squawk if I take that off the property."

"What if—if . . . you needed the kitchen towels wa-washed by tomorrow. You could say you had to do them at home. Then you could wheel me out," Lucy said.

"Why would I be in an all-fired hurry for dish towels?" the cook asked.

Lucy shrugged.

But the cook kept nodding, thinking this over. "I could call my son. He could pick the bin up in his truck. You two think up a reason he gots to take that laundry in a big hurry. And keep an eye on my onions. Only thing I got to flavor that stew." She scurried outside, across the grass to the office phone.

Ruby stirred the onions. Lucy finished mopping the pantry.

"Will you come back and visit?" Ruby asked.

Visit the orphanage? That was the last thing Lucy wanted to do.

"No," Ruby answered for Lucy.

Lucy stared at Ruby. Ruby wanted to run—Lucy could see it in her eyes—but the laundry bin wasn't big enough for two girls. Could the cook's son make two trips? It was barely believable for the cook to need one bin full of towels, but two?

Ruby waved the wooden spoon at Lucy. "What you told the other girls about that circus place. You made that up, didn't you?"

"No," Lucy said.

Ruby squinted at Lucy. "If this circus was so great, why'd you come back?"

"Mackinac and Grundy . . . caught me. F-Forced me . . . to."

Ruby searched Lucy's face. The matrons complained bitterly when more orphans arrived. Why would they go out of their way to get her back? It didn't make sense, but there was no time to explain.

Lucy took stock of Ruby's light brown skin, thick black hair, and riveting eyes. Lucy could see Ruby at Saachi's.

But Ruby needed to know Saachi's was a real place. And if she ran, she had to know where to go. Lucy felt for the route card. She didn't need it anymore, but she didn't want to part with it, either. She'd worked so hard to get it. She tightened her grip on the card.

Then she imagined telling Jabo about this. Jabo would want her to give the card to Ruby. OOFOs had to help each other.

Lucy bit her lip, then handed Ruby the card. Ruby's eyes grew large.

The door creaked open and the cook bustled back inside, her face flushed from the run. "He's coming." She smiled.

"Th-thank you!" Lucy said.

The cook nodded, her eyes glowing. "You listen to me, child. You got to find your Dilly. Now, you figured out why I need my towels in a big hurry?"

"To bake bread," Ruby said. "You cover it with a towel to make the dough rise. The towels have to be clean."

It was a good lie. Even with the cheap ingredients that made the rolls mealy, everyone loved bread. And the matrons loved the special bread the cook baked for them.

The cook nodded her approval. "Hide them clean ones, Ruby." She nodded to the stack in the pantry. "Lucy, climb in."

Lucy hopped into the old laundry cart and the cook piled the dirty laundry over her. It was dark and cold under the wet towels, and it smelled of camphor, perspiration, and mold. Lucy sneezed.

Ruby tried to push the bin, but it wouldn't roll. Lucy weighed too much for the cart.

"Don't worry none about that. My boy's a big fella. He can carry the cart." The cook's voice sounded muffled through the wet towels.

The minutes ticked by.

Lucy held her nose and tried not to sneeze again. She thought about introducing Dilly to Jabo. Riding Jenny with Dilly. Sleeping next to Dilly in the elephant car. Lucy had to find her; she just did.

Lucy's leg cramped. She moved to a more comfortable position. Her ear itched. She scratched it, then repositioned the towels over her head.

The kitchen door popped open. Heavy footsteps crossed the floor.

"Carry that one real careful. Got a child inside needs to go to the train station. Not a word about it to anyone," the cook said.

"Sure, Mama," replied a man's deep voice.

"Anybody asks, say we needed the kitchen towels for tomorrow's baking," the cook said.

Lucy felt herself tilt sideways and then rise off the ground. The cook's son shifted his weight and heaved her higher, bouncing her forward as he walked. She rocked with his swaying steps as he carried her in his swinging arms.

"And you are?" Matron Mackinac barked.

Lucy's heart stopped. Had the towels shifted? Could Mackinac see her hair so red against the white towels?

Lucy tried not to move. Not even to breathe.

"The cook's son, ma'am. She is particular about her kitchen. Won't do nothing until her towels and rags are all clean."

The cook's son had come up with his own lie.

The cook's voice was farther away. "The girls is two weeks behind on the laundry, Mrs. Mackinac. I don't have one single clean rag to work with. Can't make bread without a clean cloth. Got to cover the dough for it to rise."

"I been telling Grundy we need more girls in there." Then, in a softer voice, Mackinac said, "You go on back to the kitchen. Keep an eye on that Lucy. She's a runner."

"Yes, ma'am, will do," the cook said.

Lucy heard the rattle of the lock and the squeak of the gate as it opened.

The cook's son started walking again. He grunted as he lifted her higher, and then with a thump dropped the cart onto a truck bed. She could hear the sharp bleep of a car horn, the tweeting of birds, the river burbling over the stones in the distance.

And then a minute later *shugety-shug, shugety-shug,* the truck moved forward. She heard the whoosh of passing cars. She wanted to peek out, but she didn't dare.

A few minutes later the truck jolted to a stop. The cab door opened, then shut. Lucy stiffened when the hands pulled the towels off her. But it was the big smiling face of the cook's son, with his thick black mustache and his mama's lively eyes.

"All righty, little girl. This is the train station. I gotta run. I'm late for work. You gonna be okay here?"

She nodded.

"Good luck to you," he said, and he was gone.

CHAPTER THIRTY-ONE

LAST TRAIN TO CHICAGO

Lucy pulled open the door to the train station lobby and a huge press of stale, hot air swelled around her.

People were getting off trains. People were getting on trains. People were waiting with bags, baskets, and suitcases, drinking pop from bottles, reading newspapers, and bustling out to platforms.

Lucy searched the waiting area, the ticket lines, the benches, even the ladies' room.

No Dilly.

Lucy kept her eye on the doors, watching everyone who came in.

Would Dilly come? Had she already left?

Lucy searched the platforms again. But there was no one

with curly red hair, a determined step, and a laugh you could hear a block away.

She waited in line at the ticket counter to ask which train went to Chicago. The man behind the counter had a plaid vest, red ears, and a bow tie. He couldn't have been friendlier. Even so, the old panic struck. Lucy wrote quickly. *Last train to Chicago?*

"Leaves at five o'clock. Platform three." He squinted at her. "You want a ticket, missy?"

Lucy shook her head, then ran to platform three, but the train hadn't arrived. She ran back to a bench behind a pillar. This was a good spot to watch for Dilly and watch out for Mackinac and Grundy. She could keep an eye on the train platforms from here, too.

How much time did she have before Mackinac noticed Lucy was gone? How much before they checked the train station?

Lucy's eyes were on the door, the train, the big clock on the wall.

Four-fifteen. A family with seven blond girls came through the doors.

Four-seventeen. A lady with lots of luggage.

Four-thirty. A crowd of men in suits.

Four-thirty-two. The train arrived on platform three. Out to the platform she ran.

Four-forty-two. Back to the pillar.

Maybe the cook heard wrong. Maybe she got the day mixed up. Maybe Dilly was leaving from a different train station. Maybe she'd gotten a ride in an automobile. Maybe she was planning to take a train tomorrow. Maybe it hadn't been Dilly at all.

No, that couldn't be true. No one but Dilly would cry when they saw Mrs. Three Eyes.

"Last call for Chicago," the ticket man shouted.

Lucy ran closer to the train.

"All aboard," the conductor called. She watched the last three passengers board.

Then the whistle blew. A minute later the train began to move. *Chickety-chickety-chickety* along the tracks.

Lucy's feet were heavy in her shoes. Her heart heavier still.

Then she took a deep breath and tried to think what to do.

She'd go back to Saachi's. Nico, Eugene, Jabo, Grace, Bunk, Nitty-Bitty, Baby, Jenny, even Bald Doris were family now. She'd look for Dilly when they performed in Chicago, as she had planned before.

Nico had gotten her chances back. Grace had given her an apprenticeship. Jabo would know what had gone wrong with Diavolo and how she could make things right.

All she needed was money for the train ticket to New Brownsville, where Saachi's would be going tonight. She went to talk to the man behind the counter. But the mean voice in her head came back.

Dilly doesn't care about you. Nobody does.

Lucy knew this was Miss Holland and Matron Mackinac in her head. But they weren't here. The voice was hers now.

There was a line behind her. No time to write. She took a wobbly breath but could force no words out.

A shadow passed over the ticket man's face.

He sees how stupid you are.

Lucy dug her nails into her leg. She could ride an elephant. She'd made Grace proud of her and she was Bunk's favorite OOFO. "How . . . how much . . . to take the tr-train to New Brownsville?" she asked.

"I thought you were going to Chicago?" the ticket man said.

"I was j-just . . . curious."

The ticket man nodded. "$1.20. It leaves at six."

"Thank you." The words pounded out strong and clear.

In the train station in Chicago, there had been people who sang or played music for money. They had placed an upside-down hat in front of them and passersby had dropped coins inside.

Lucy didn't have a hat, but she took off the apron the cook had given her, folded it into a square in front of her, and wrote, *Need money to go home.*

Then she began to sing. She sang the songs Dilly liked from the radio at the Sokoloffs and coins began to drop noiselessly into the apron.

The coins came faster as she found her rhythm. And faster still when she began to dance. All the while, she kept one eye out for Dilly just in case, and another for Mackinac.

It was five-fifteen.

Then five-thirty. Now the nickels were clinking against each other.

She counted the money. Just ten cents to go. She kept singing, watching the people walking by. But no more coins dropped in.

April 24, 1939
Home for Friendless Children
Riverport, Iowa

Dear Mrs. Mackinac,

I am all broken into pieces. I had every hope of finding my Lucy. At least now I know she passed away peacefully.

But if there is another girl who is searching for her sister, please tell her the truth from the start. It isn't right to get a girl's hopes up so she believes with everything inside her that she will see her sister again.

Thank you for giving me the doll I made for my sister. It is the only thing I have from her. Mrs. Three Eyes and I will get on the train to Chicago more brokenhearted than you can ever know.

Yours truly,
Dilly Sauvé

April 24, 1939

Dear Lucy,

Mrs. Sokoloff would say I'm crazy, meshugga, for writing to a person who has passed away. But there are so many things I wanted to say to you & this is the only way I can do it now.

You were the best sister & I am sorry I bossed you around and fought with you about who got the good chair. When we lived together I didn't appreciate how special it is to have a sister.

I have been thinking on what I loved best about you & I think it was how excited you got about every little thing & how you would read out loud to me & how you skipped everywhere. Mama would tell you to settle down and you would for a little while and then before we knew it you would be skipping and hopping again.

I don't know what makes a person matter to another person. But there have never been people who matter to me like you and Mama. I'm terribly wretched to be without you both. This life is cold as stone. I can't believe I didn't find you until it was too late.

Love,
Dilly

April 25, 1939

Dear Mrs. Mackinac,

I am sitting here on a bench outside the train
station, because I heard a beggar girl singing inside.
Her voice made me feel so broke up, I couldn't set one
foot in there.

I'm early for my train. It goes roundabout to
Chicago. The ticket was cheaper that way. By the time
the train is here, I'm hoping the beggar girl will be
gone. It causes me terrible pain to hear a girl sing who
sounds so much like my Lucy did.

But this is not why I am writing. I went to the
cemetery after I saw you. I wanted to say goodbye
to my Lucy, but I couldn't find where she was buried.
I met a man tending the flowers. I asked him if he
knew where Lucy's grave was. He did not.

I walked all over reading tombstones. I found
gravestone markers that read UNKNOWN ORPHAN,
but no headstone said Lucy Sauvé.

My Lucy was not an UNKNOWN ORPHAN.
She was Lucy Simone Sauvé, and I want her to have a
proper marker that says her name so all the world will
know my Lucy was here.

I have checked with an engraver and he has let me
know how much $$ this will cost. I will go home &

earn the $$ to send to him. But I will need your help to know which is Lucy's grave. Please could you send me her exact grave location as soon as possible.

Yours truly,

Dilly Sauvé

CHAPTER THIRTY-TWO

WOMAN IN RED

It was ten minutes to six when a man in a gray suit tossed in the last dime.

"Th-thank you!" Lucy cried. Then she rolled the money inside the apron and took off for the ticket line. The ticket-counter man winked at her when she gave him the money with her note that said *New Brownsville*.

"You got a lovely voice. My brother's the postman. He told me about an orphan sang so beautiful he bought her stamps out of his own pocket. 'Voice like an angel,' he said. That wouldn't be you, would it?"

Lucy grinned.

"Well, aren't you the one. Thanks for making my afternoon, little missy. Platform seven. Better hurry. Leaves in eight minutes."

Lucy raced to platform seven and got in line behind a lady carrying two large suitcases and a man with a big trunk. She was waiting patiently for them to get on when she spotted Mackinac and Grundy in their gray hats and gray sweaters.

Lucy ducked behind the train. When she peeked out, she saw that the passengers with all the luggage had filed up the stairs. Then she ran around the train and scrambled aboard.

Inside, Lucy found a seat in the back and slid down low, her heart beating loud as Nitty-Bitty's supper gong. Had Mackinac or Grundy seen her? Would they come on board and drag her off?

If only the train would leave now, then she'd be safe.

Lucy peeked out the window.

No Mackinac or Grundy. But there was a woman in a red coat walking from the platform. She was tall and slender like Dilly, and she had the Sauvés' red hair!

Lucy's heart swelled. She rushed down the aisle and through the vestibule and leapt onto the platform.

"Dilly!" She chased after the woman in red. "D-Dilly!" Her legs pumped, blood rushing through her.

Dilly was inside the lobby by the time Lucy caught her and grabbed her arm.

Dilly spun around.

But the lady had blue eyes and glasses and a large nose. She wasn't Dilly.

"Excuse m-me. S-s-sorry," Lucy mumbled. "I thought you w-were someone else."

The train!

Lucy sprinted back to platform seven, slamming past the ticket man, who was out of his ticket cage. "Be careful—those orphanage ladies are looking for you," he called after her.

At the platform, her train was moving.

"Wait! Wait! I h-have a ticket!" Lucy ran after the train, waving her ticket in the air.

Lucy's fingers grazed the metal side of the train, but she couldn't get a grip. The train picked up speed. She ran faster.

Down the tracks the train flew.

Lucy could not keep up. All she could do was watch it go.

CHAPTER THIRTY-THREE

"WARD OF THE STATE"

Lucy ran back to the lobby looking for the nice ticket seller to explain what happened. Maybe she could exchange her ticket for a ticket on a later train. But coming out of the ladies' room was Mackinac.

Lucy careened around a pole and leapt over a folded-up newspaper, her feet pounding the floor. She was bolting toward the front entrance, when she saw the suitcase.

It was old and brown and held together by a belt because one brass clasp was missing. The corner was dented, and there was a gash on the side where an iron had fallen on it.

Lucy's heart caught in her throat.

The suitcase looked like the one that had been in the Sokoloffs' apartment. It had held their precious phonograph records. She and Dilly had been allowed to look through them and pick one to play.

It was only a suitcase. There were lots of suitcases like this. Lucy tried to make herself run, but her breath caught and her legs froze.

An old man in a rumpled suit stood in the ticket line, then a businessman with a briefcase, then a woman in a worn brown coat. The woman's hair was tucked under a hat, but something about her rounded shoulders was achingly familiar. Lucy tried to call out, but her throat had closed up.

She swallowed hard. "D-Dilly."

The woman didn't turn around.

But now Mackinac had seen Lucy. She charged toward her from one direction, Grundy from another.

Lucy's feet were planted. She grabbed the lady's coat sleeve.

The lady wheeled around.

Lucy gasped.

"Mama!"

Mama with deep circles under her eyes.

Then she recognized Dilly's blue eyes and slender nose. Dilly had grown up to look like Mama.

Dilly jumped from the window, the ticket still on the counter. She wrapped her long bony arms around Lucy, her shoulders trembling.

"Excuse me," Matron Mackinac barked, pushing her big chest forward. "But that orphan is a ward of the state."

Dilly's eyes nearly popped out of her face.

"You! You told me she was dead, Mrs. Mackinac!" Dilly roared. "How dare you!"

"Evidently we were mistaken," Mrs. Mackinac said. "But that doesn't mean we can allow—"

"She's not an orphan. She's my sister, and no one is going to take her from me! Stay away. Do you hear me?"

"Well," Matron Mackinac huffed. "You don't have the proper paperwork to take her."

"You've lied to me. You've tricked me. You've sent me on one wild-goose chase after another. You've given me nothing but tsuris."

"I beg your pardon," Matron Mackinac said.

"You got too many children to feed at that orphanage. Those girls are thin as matchsticks. Why would you want to keep my sister from me?" Dilly stood between Lucy and Mackinac.

"Excuse me. We've done nothing of the kind. We do the best we can with our meager resources."

"No—no you don't!" Lucy shouted. "You spend all the money on the matrons' food."

"Lucy. Children are to be seen and not heard," Mackinac hissed. "See"—she pointed an accusing finger at Dilly—"we try to raise our children to be respectful, but people like you come along allowing back talk and bad manners."

"You are nothing b-but mean," Lucy said.

Mackinac's small gray eyes turned dark. She sidestepped Dilly to slap Lucy.

But Lucy ducked and Mackinac missed.

Matron Grundy stepped up, her spine straight and her gray bun pulled tight. "Miss Sauvé," she said, "we don't have any proof you are who you say you are. We can't let our girls go with just any person—"

"She's . . . D-Dilly! My sister!" Lucy cried.

"Did you think she wouldn't know her own sister?" Dilly asked.

The ticket seller joined the small crowd around them. "These are nice girls, Mrs. Mackinac. You let them be."

"Go on back and take care of the ones who need you," a man with a gray mustache and thick glasses said.

"Anybody can see by looking at them they're sisters," the ticket seller said.

"They've got each other. The older one can take care of the two of them. Can't you, dear?" a lady in a blue hat asked Dilly.

"Yes, ma'am. I make enough money to take good care of the both of us," Dilly said proudly.

"There now, Hannah Mackinac. Your work here is done," the lady with the blue hat said. "You go on back to the orphans who need you."

Matrons Mackinac and Grundy stood rooted to the ground. "I'm afraid you don't understand the full extent of the problem—" Mackinac began.

"I tell you one thing," the man in the business suit interrupted, "taxpayers pay for that orphanage. No sense in having a girl there who doesn't need to be."

"It's a blessing these sisters have each other, dearie. I don't see what else there is to know," the lady with the blue hat said.

Mackinac crossed her arms, her neck set.

"Hannah," Matron Grundy whispered, trying to catch Mackinac's eye.

Mackinac ignored her.

Matron Grundy offered a mealy smile to the townspeople and walked outside. Mackinac stood firm, but the people in the station had formed a ring around Lucy and Dilly. They were not about to back down.

"This isn't the proper way to handle this," Mackinac insisted, wiping beads of sweat off her forehead.

Nobody paid any attention to her, and soon she stomped out the door.

When she was gone, the ticket seller smiled from one large red ear to the other and the little crowd cheered.

"I can't wait to tell my brother about the excitement we had here today," the ticket seller said.

"Oh, how I love a happy ending," the lady with the blue hat sighed.

Dilly wrapped her arms around Lucy and didn't let go. Lucy hadn't been hugged like this in such a long time, but the memory was vivid, the years together more powerful than the years apart.

Dilly had come.

CHAPTER THIRTY-FOUR

"YOU WERE ALWAYS SUCH A CHATTERBOX."

Every time Lucy blinked she worried Dilly would disappear. But she didn't disappear. It wasn't a dream. Dilly was really here.

Lucy took Dilly's hand and held it tightly.

Their bond was blood and bone and breath and something deeper than that. Sisters can be separated, but they can't be torn apart.

They sat on the bench outside the train station, too overcome to move. Lucy had imagined seeing Dilly a million times, but in her mind's eye Dilly was the old Dilly, not this new grown-up person. Seeing her made the ache of missing Mama deeper.

Together they watched the night falling and the lights begin to flicker on.

At last, Lucy ran her hands over the old suitcase. "What . . . happened to the S-Sokoloffs?"

"Nothing. They're fine. I live with them. After you left, we moved in with their daughter. I went to school and then last year I got a job. I'm a seamstress now."

"Like Mama."

Dilly's eyes filled up again.

"Do you ever wonder what would have happened . . . if she hadn't ever met Th-Thomas Slater?" Lucy asked.

"We would have stayed together and been happy," Dilly said.

"Remember how Mama was sure he had a closet full of—of f-fancy suits."

Dilly nodded.

"He only had one suit . . . the blue one," Lucy said.

"What was his house like?"

"A r-room . . . in a broken-down hotel."

Dilly sighed. "I knew he wasn't rich. I told Mama."

Lucy nodded.

"I wrote Thomas Slater letter after letter asking where you were. Never heard back." Dilly's voice was tight. "Finally this year I got a letter Mama wrote five years ago. Mama's letter said you were at the Home for Friendless Children. I'll show you when we get home. But Mackinac said you weren't there."

"They d-didn't want you to find me."

"I know, but why?"

"They n-needed me. I was in a study . . . at the university.

They wanted to see if they could turn me into a st-stutterer. The university paid them."

"What? Why would anyone do a study like that?"

"To understand how kids become stutterers. I st-stopped talking because—because every time I opened my mouth they t-told me how badly I stuttered. I didn't stutter . . . before the study. You remember?"

Dilly nodded, her eyes bulging with anger. Her fists clenched.

"I was wondering what happened. You were always such a chatterbox. You never stumbled over your words."

Lucy nodded.

Dilly sighed, her eyes focused on a faraway porch light. A train whistle blew. The wind rustled the leaves of a nearby tree. "I don't even know how to think about that, it's so wrong."

Lucy knew this, but it felt good to have Dilly say it. To have it matter so much to her. Lucy wasn't alone in the world anymore.

• • • • • • • • • • • • • • • • • • • •
CHAPTER THIRTY-FIVE
• • • • • • • • • • • • • • • • • • • •

"FROM WHEN WE WERE LITTLE"

Dilly rubbed the goose bumps on Lucy's arms. "You're getting cold. Let's go back to the boardinghouse where I stayed last night."

Dilly got the Sokoloffs' suitcase and they made their way down the tree-lined street to town.

As they walked, Lucy wondered how to tell Dilly about the circus. What would Dilly make of Bald Doris, Nico, Eugene, Jabo, Grace, and the roustabouts? What would she think of the elephants?

Lucy worried there would be no one Dilly's age for her to be friends with. She fretted about whether Dilly would like the costume shop. She wondered if Dilly would like living in a train car. And she tried to block the one question she couldn't answer.

What if Dilly didn't want to join the circus?

When Dilly rang the boardinghouse bell, a lady with long dark eyelashes and soft old lady skin stuck her head out. The lady nodded to Dilly, then her eyes traveled to Lucy. "You found her! She's alive!"

Dilly beamed.

"And don't you two look alike. Two peas in a pod. Oh my, you got me so excited I think I'm going to have to sit myself down." She backed into the house and collapsed onto a pink chair.

Dilly and Lucy followed her into the living room, which was full of dolls and porcelain animals. Every surface was covered with a doily, and the lampshades all had fringe.

The lady shook her head at Dilly. "Aren't you something," she said.

"Would it be okay if I used your phone?" Dilly asked. "I'll pay you." Dilly handed the lady money for the phone call and for one more night's stay. "Do you need any more mending done?"

The boardinghouse lady scratched one leg with the stockinged foot of the other. "I got an invite to the church women's luncheon and I don't have anything to wear. Don't suppose you could help me with that?"

"Oh yes, ma'am," Dilly said, following her up the stairs.

When Dilly came back down, she was carrying a blue housecoat. Lucy followed her into a bedroom that had a quilted bedspread, a desk, and a sewing machine.

Dilly unbuckled her suitcase, pulled out Mrs. Three Eyes, and handed her to Lucy.

How she had longed for Mrs. Three Eyes that first year at the orphanage. Lucy couldn't believe how good it felt to hold her again.

Lucy hugged the old doll. Then she pulled the doll's button nose out of her pocket and set it on the doll's face.

Dilly grinned when she saw it. "Shall I sew it back on?" she asked.

Lucy shook her head. Her pocket didn't feel right without it. "N-not yet."

Dilly understood. Of course she did. She was Dilly.

Then Lucy took out her baby tooth and handed it to her sister.

"What's this? Oh . . . your tooth. Remember when you lost your first one?"

Lucy nodded.

"Mama had to pull it out with a thread. Then she kept it in her pin box. She had mine, too. She said she wanted to keep a piece of us from when we were little."

Lucy's chest welled up. The tooth had been so important to her. Until now she hadn't remembered why.

"I'll keep it for you, okay?" Dilly whispered.

Lucy nodded, wiping her eyes. Then she climbed into the bed with the doll and sat watching Dilly sketch out a new skirt. But the day had been long and the pillow was fluffy and soft.

Lucy awoke a few hours later to the sound of the whirring sewing machine. There was Dilly hunched over her work, just like Mama.

In the morning, Dilly had fashioned a smart blue skirt from the old housecoat.

"It's . . . beautiful," Lucy said. "If only Ma-Mama could see. She would be proud."

"Hush, you're going to make me start blubbering again," Dilly said, dabbing at her eyes.

The boardinghouse lady was so happy with the skirt, she flip-flopped over to her neighbor's in her slippers to show her. When she returned, she gave back the money Dilly had paid her the night before.

Back in their room, Dilly strapped the Sokoloffs' suitcase closed. Lucy knew she had to tell Dilly about the circus now, but before she could get the words out, Dilly said, "There's something else I need to say. Something I feel awful about."

Lucy turned toward her.

"I could have gone with you and Mama. The Sokoloffs offered to lend me money for the train ticket. But I was so mad at Mama I didn't want to go." Dilly took a ragged breath. "I could have taken care of you and Mama, but I let my temper get the best of me. The last time Mama saw me I was shouting at her."

Lucy hugged her. "You were twelve. Thomas Slater would have . . . p-put you in the orphanage, too."

"I wish I had it to do over again. I'm so sorry, Lucy."

"We don't know what would have happened. It might have been w-worse."

Dilly nodded. "Maybe. But I shouldn't have behaved like that. I just couldn't understand why Mama chose Thomas Slater."

"She l-loved him, Dil," Lucy said, thinking of what Bunk said once. "You love . . . who you love," she whispered.

"I'm not going to fall in love with anyone like that. And you better not, either." She wagged her finger at Lucy.

"I . . . I won't," Lucy said.

Dilly stood up and buckled the suitcase. "Okay, let's go home."

"Wait . . . Dilly . . . ," Lucy said.

Dilly arched an eyebrow. "What?"

"I . . . I . . . h-have a job. I'm elephant girl . . . at Saachi's . . . Circus Spec-Spectacular."

Dilly's face screwed up. "What?"

Lucy dug in her pocket for the silk purse with the elephant hairs and handed them to Dilly. Dilly untied the little drawstring and pulled the coiled hairs out.

"Elephant-t-tail hairs," Lucy explained. "I'm an apprentice to Lady Grace, the strongest woman in the entire world, and she's in charge of the menagerie, except—except she spends all her time with the elephants because she loves Baby."

On and on Lucy talked about the elephants, the cook tent, the roustabouts, Jabo, the OOFOs, and the Elephantoff act. She told Dilly about Eugene, Bald Doris, Nico, and how they'd all gotten their apprenticeships. And how she had finally convinced Grace to take her on.

Dilly shifted from foot to foot, her eyes on the door. "It sounds special, but I have a job waiting for me. We can live with the Sokoloffs and you can go to school. I called them last night. They can't wait to see you!"

"You can work in the costume shop. Betts, she's the seamstress and she's pregnant. She needs help." Lucy was breathless trying to get it all in. "You should see—see the costumes. They are more beautiful than anything you've ever sewn before."

Dilly frowned. "People don't just hand you jobs, Lucy."

"I saw . . . saw what you did with that skirt."

Dilly smiled. Her eyes shone.

"And there's a schoolroom for circus kids, and, and, and . . ." Whenever Dilly opened her mouth, Lucy spoke faster.

Dilly gave up and sat back down.

Lucy talked and talked until her throat hurt. Then she stared out the window. But she couldn't see the river, only the brick wall of the house next door.

A silence fell between them.

"You'll love Saachi's," Lucy said.

A crease appeared between Dilly's brows.

"I'm an . . . apprentice. I w-worked hard for this. Come see it with me. Please!"

Dilly sighed. "When you talk about the circus, you speak more like how you used to. We could never shut you up."

Lucy grinned. "Is that a y-yes?"

Dilly held her hand up. Lucy stopped.

"Whatever they did to you, those study people . . ." Dilly's face hardened and her voice trailed off. "It's getting better at this circus place?"

Lucy nodded.

"What makes you think this Betts person will give me a job?"

"She needs a seamstress."

"Maybe they've hired someone already."

"Maybe they . . . h-haven't."

Dilly crossed her eyes at Lucy. "I forgot how stubborn you are."

Lucy smiled. "I forgot how stubborn you—you are."

Dilly laughed. "Well, you know what we used to do . . . ask Mrs. Three Eyes."

Lucy dug in the suitcase for the rag doll and handed it to Dilly.

"What do you think, Mrs. Three Eyes? Shall we go to the circus?" Dilly asked.

Lucy held her breath.

Mrs. Three Eyes's head didn't move.

"She's thinking," Dilly explained. Then Dilly's fingers made the rag doll's head nod once, then twice. "She says so long as you agree we go back to Chicago if it doesn't work out."

"Oh, it's going to w-work out," Lucy said. It had to work out. Lucy couldn't imagine it any other way.

Dilly said nothing at first; then she whispered in a gentle voice, "How long were you even there, Lucy?"

"Dilly, p-please, you have to . . . believe me." Lucy watched Dilly put on her coat.

"I do," Dilly said, "But if I can't get a job there, we're going back, right?"

Lucy took Mrs. Three Eyes from Dilly and made her head nod yes.

CHAPTER THIRTY-SIX

SAWDUST IN HER SHOES

Lucy breathed in the smell of leftover cigarette smoke and egg-salad sandwich. She stared out the train window as they rattled through the farmland. They'd caught an early train and would be in New Brownsville soon.

Lucy hadn't said anything to Dilly about Diavolo. She knew she should have. But Dilly had barely agreed to come as it was.

Dilly was such a sensible person and here Lucy was asking her to do something she thought was completely crazy. Dilly was spending her last dollars to go to the circus, because Lucy wanted her to.

Sisters were different from friends. They did things for you no one else would.

*　*　*

When they pulled into the town before New Brownsville, Lucy saw the first circus bill pasted on a telephone pole. She jumped out of her seat. "D-Dilly, look! That's us!"

But the poster flew by so quickly, Dilly didn't see it.

A minute later they passed another and another. Then an entire wall plastered with circus posters. Elephantoff in her hair salon, monkeys riding bicycles, the acrobat family, and Diavolo. Dilly drew an uneasy breath and squeezed Lucy's hand.

"Next stop, New Brownsville," the conductor called.

Lucy jumped up and ran down the aisle. Dilly followed, the Sokoloffs' suitcase knocking against her legs.

Ding, ding, ding, the train rolled through a crossing and into a small brick station. The engines chuffed and hissed as the train came to a stop. Lucy rushed on to the vestibule and dashed down the steps.

She had hoped they would arrive just in time for the performance. Nico would get Dilly a ticket, and she would sit in the stands and watch the show. Then, once the performance was over and the circus magic had worked its charm on Dilly, Lucy would introduce Dilly to Jabo.

But it was only nine-thirty. The train trip had been short. The performance wouldn't start until two.

Lucy didn't want Dilly to think about how much work was involved in putting up a circus early in the morning and taking it down in the evening. She wanted Dilly to see the beauty of the circus, not the work. The work wouldn't matter if Dilly had sawdust in her shoes, but if she didn't . . .

Lucy and Dilly took turns carrying the Sokoloffs' suitcase down the rutted road. When they crested the hill, they saw the circus. The cook tent was up. The big top. The ticket booth. Lucy ran. Dilly ran after her.

The first person Lucy saw was a man she didn't know carrying crates of vegetables. Her stomach clenched when she remembered the roustabout who had forced her into the old blue Ford.

But the man didn't give them a second glance. When they got to the parking area, Lucy saw the town kids who came early hoping to earn a free ticket in exchange for helping out.

Then she spotted a fuzzy blond head.

Doris charged forward and hugged Lucy. "Did you go back to the orphanage? Did you tell them about me?"

Lucy nodded.

"What did they say?"

"They didn't believe . . . wh-what I said."

Doris's shoulders fell. "Why not?"

"You w-wouldn't believe it either if you still . . . if you still lived there."

"But you always tell the truth. They know that."

Lucy shrugged.

"Hey"—Doris frowned at Lucy—"It wasn't my fault. I told Diavolo about Frank, just like Nico said."

Lucy scrutinized Doris.

"Diavolo forgot to tell the roustabouts who work for him not to help Mackinac. You believe me, right?"

Lucy didn't know what to say. Sometimes she could tell when Doris was lying and sometimes she couldn't.

"Jeez, Lucy," Doris growled, "what's the point of being good when everyone thinks it's always me who messed up?"

Lucy bit her lip so she wouldn't smile. Now she knew Doris was telling the truth.

"Listen," Doris said, and sighed in a big, important way, "Diavolo had already called Mackinac to come get you because you'd lost your chances. Then he called her back and told her not to come, but she came anyway."

Lucy nodded.

Doris stared at Dilly. "Who are *you*? Wait . . ."

Dilly held out her hand. "I'm Dilly Sauvé."

Doris gaped at Lucy. "You found Dilly!"

Lucy grinned. Then she saw pain shoot through Doris's face.

"Well, I could find my mama too, you know. I just haven't tried," Doris announced.

Once at the orphanage a mama had come back to get her little girl. Oh, how Lucy and the other girls had cried when they saw the mama hug her girl. Lucy squeezed Doris's hand.

"Let's find Diavolo," Doris said. "You'll need to check in with him. I get to wear the target-girl dress, but I don't have to be his target. I just hand him his knives. I look pretty and I don't have to wear clown trousers!"

Dilly stood awkwardly, holding the suitcase.

"I'll explain la-later," Lucy whispered, grabbing Dilly's

hand and pulling her along behind Doris. They went straight to the ticket booth, where Diavolo was pacing.

His eyebrows popped up when he saw Lucy.

Lucy's heart began to race. She forced her mouth open. "Diavolo, sir . . . um, sir. This . . . is Dilly . . . my sister. She is a s-seamstress. She's come to . . . help you with your costume. I know it's—it's never fit right."

Diavolo peered at Dilly. "A seamstress, you say?"

"Yes, sir," Dilly said.

"Are you fast?"

"Oh yes, sir."

"The vest is too tight across my shoulders. It inhibits my range of motion. But it can't be too loose. I need support. A steadying firmness." Diavolo moved his hands when he talked.

"I've got a good eye for fit, sir," Dilly said. "I'll get it right if you give me a chance."

Lucy felt a surge of pride. If anyone could get that vest to fit the way Diavolo wanted, it would be her big sister.

Diavolo nodded, then turned his attention to Lucy. "You"—he pointed his finger at her—"have caused me all kinds of trouble."

Lucy gulped, her eyes on Doris.

"Seraphina bit my head off. Bunk threatened to quit. Jabo turned the entire dwarf population against me. Nitty-Bitty burnt my toast!" He glared at Lucy.

"B-but . . . ," Lucy started.

"I called those orphanage women. Mrs. Mackinac and Mrs. Grundy. I told them not to come. But they were bound and determined. I couldn't change their minds. So why was your disappearing my fault?"

"I told you," Doris whispered.

"Everybody blamed me. Me!" Diavolo said.

"I'm s-sorry," Lucy whispered.

"You were the one who lost her chances." He pointed at her. "Don't put me in that kind of a situation again. Do you hear?"

"Yes, sir," Lucy said.

"I'll make sure Mrs. Mackinac and Mrs. Grundy don't go near her again," Dilly said.

Diavolo nodded to Dilly. "Good. That's good. Now you, seamstress, come with me. And, Doris, I need my water half-filled with ice."

Dilly tilted her head at Lucy, her eyes full of questions. Then she followed Diavolo.

Diavolo was the last person Lucy wanted to introduce Dilly to Saachi's. But Dilly had clever fingers. She could sew her way out of any situation. If only Diavolo would be nice.

Doris headed for the cook tent and Lucy ran to the menagerie. The backyard was set up the same at every stand, so it was easy to find her way around. When Lucy got close, she heard the elephants trumpeting. She ran faster, plowing through the door of the menagerie tent, which smelled of al-falfa and apple and the elephants' warm, sweet breath.

She was home.

Baby saw her first. She made gurgling sounds and stretched her trunk out to Lucy. Jenny stood solemnly while Lucy hugged her, then patted her wrinkled cheeks.

Grace looked up from raking. "What happened to you?"

"The orphanage l-ladies forced me to go back."

"That's what Jabo thought."

"But I g-got away."

"Of course you did. You're my elephant girl. I want to hear all about it. But right now we have work to do."

Lucy had just hooked on coveralls over her dress when Nico came thundering in.

He ran to her, picked her up, and swung her around. Then he let go, his face pink.

"I had it all planned. I was going to come get you. We've got a stand in Wilbur. That's the next town over from River-port. Gonna look for Willy, too," Nico whispered.

"I didn't . . . see him. I don't know if he's—he's there."

Nico nodded.

"There's a g-girl . . . she helped me. Ruby."

"We'll get her too," Nico said. "Is it true you found Dilly?"

Lucy grinned.

"Does she look like you?" Nico asked.

"I g-guess."

"She's beautiful, then," Nico said.

Grace looked up from where she was cleaning Jenny's short tusks. "Nico, you're making a nuisance of yourself. Go on, get out of here. Lucy's got work to do!"

"Yes, ma'am," Nico said.

"That boy is smitten," Grace muttered when Nico had gone. "Bunk dared him to go one whole meal without mentioning your name. Couldn't do it."

Lucy smiled as she cleaned the elephant area, washed Jenny, and massaged ointment into Baby's legs. It felt so good to be working with them again. She even found herself talking to them—well, whispering, anyway, so only they could hear. When the midday meal gong sounded, she slipped off her coveralls and sped to the costume shop, where Dilly had her head bent over a sewing machine and her hands working on something shiny and red.

"How's it . . . going?" Lucy gasped, out of breath from the run.

Dilly's head popped up. "Some of the liberty horse girls gain weight on the road. We have to make their costumes forgiving or by Minnesota they can't get them on. The aerialist has skin allergies. She can only wear cotton. The band coats can't be lined. The band pit gets warm in the summer and the trumpet player is prone to fainting. Oh yeah, and we worked out Diavolo's vest problem."

We. Dilly had said *we.*

"I like Betts. . . ." Dilly dropped her voice to a whisper. "And I'm pretty sure she likes me. You found nice people, Lucy. I like it here."

Lucy jumped on Dilly, hugging her tightly.

Dilly laughed. "Never thought I'd be sewing costumes for a monkey." She held up a tiny red-spangled outfit. "What would Mama say?"

May 1, 1939
R&M Dresses
Chicago, Illinois

Dear Mrs. LaFinestre,

Thank you for holding my job, but I won't need it anymore.

In this world that can be terribly hard & unkind, there are miracles, and one of them happened to me. I found my little sister, and the aching hole of missing her is gone.

I'm sorry I can't return to machine #71 & prove how grateful I am. Please know I have thought real hard on this. And the plan I have come up with to thank you for what you did is to pass your kindness on to another girl. I will let her use the good machine, the black one where I work now at the costume shop of Saachi's Circus. I will give her time off, when she needs it. And I will always leave the light on for her, like you did for me.

> Yours truly,
> Dilly Sauvé

P.S. Please tell the girl on #71 to oil the presser foot lift and change the bobbin thread before it runs out. #71 does not like being run with an empty bobbin.

May 5, 1939

Dear Mama,

The sky is big. I don't know if you can see me from where you are, but I wave up at you every night.

I've been missing you a lot lately, so Dilly said I should write.

Dilly and I found each other, did you know that?

Dilly had been trying so hard to find me and I had been trying so hard to find her that when we finally found each other, we just sat and cried. Dilly's hankie got so wet we had to wring it out in the sink.

Dilly is so much like you, Mama. The way she lines up her pins in her sleeve and holds the needle to the light to thread. The way she clicks her tongue when she's adding numbers, puts vanilla on our pillowcases, and unpins her hair to brush it at night.

We work at Saachi's Circus Spectacular. Dilly sews costumes and I take care of the elephants. This morning Dilly sewed matching tuxedos for Tiny, the Great Dane, and for the tramp clown's Chihuahua. How we laughed watching the giant black-and-white dog and the itty-bitty brown one strut around in their coats and bow ties.

Yesterday, Grace let me help with Baby's new act. Baby is dressed up as a housewife with lots of cleaning to do and a rag-doll baby who won't stop crying. I wonder what you would say if you saw me teaching an elephant to vacuum.

Dilly has become friends with Betts the seamstress and Bernadette, who visits when she can. I'm best friends with Nico, Eugene, Jabo, Grace, and Bunk. I don't know if I'm friends with Doris or not. She is good at making people laugh, but I don't trust her and sometimes I don't like her, though when she's not around, I miss her a lot. Have you ever had a friend like that?

Every day, we work and do lessons at school. Our teacher is Jabo. He teaches us with riddles, puzzles, and tricks.

At night, we sleep on the train. Sometimes Dilly sleeps in the elephant car with Nico, Doris, Eugene, and me. Other times in the single-lady car, with stockings hanging from the berths, radios playing dance music, and girls gossiping about who dates who. (Dilly doesn't date, but she turns pink and stares at her feet when a certain acrobat walks by.)

At meals, we sit together in the cook tent with Bunk, Rib, and Nevada. When Dilly first sat with us, she didn't join in their kidding. But then Bunk discovered Dilly had a dimple in her left cheek and he simply had to see it. Now he makes her laugh every day.

I still have trouble speaking, and some days I don't want to talk. Dilly is furious at Miss Holland and

Mrs. Mackinac for how they treated me. She says she's going to write letters to the newspapers about what they did. I'm angry too, though mostly at myself, for letting their meanness get up inside me. But every day with Dilly, the elephants, and my friends, it gets better.

I love having Dilly here. It's the best thing that's ever happened to me. But she is so much like you, she makes me miss you more.

Dilly says when we talk about you, you stay alive inside us, and when we wave up at you, you wave down. Jabo says that your love is in the air we breathe. Bunk says to close my eyes and you will come.

I hope you and Papa can see us. I hope you're proud of Dilly and me.

Love,

Lucy

AUTHOR'S NOTE

· ·

I fancy myself an elephant whisperer. In another life, I was a pachyderm.

In 2017, I traveled to Chiang Mai, Thailand, to visit four elephant sanctuaries and get up close and personal with elephants. It was the trip of a lifetime, and some of the descriptions of Jenny and Baby came directly from my journals of that trip. A portion of the proceeds of this book will be donated to savetheelephants.org. I believe this organization is among those doing the most to protect these incredible animals.

In 2018, I attended the annual Circus Historical Society Convention in Baraboo, Wisconsin. I'm obsessed with circus history. I read everything I can get my hands on about it. Getting to rub elbows with luminaries in the circus historical field was an incredible experience.

Saachi's Circus Spectacular is fictional, though I worked hard to create an authentic 1939 circus feel for this book. That said, I did take creative license. Jabo's apprenticeship system and his OOFO organization are complete fabrications. Also, in the circus of 1939, people with dwarfism would probably have been called midgets. Since today this is a derogatory term, I used the term "dwarf," or on occasion "little person." Both are acceptable names for people of short stature, according to the Little Persons Association.[1] Though the term "little person" is more contemporary, it also is an obvious description, which could easily have been used in 1939.

Many people who did not fit into the narrow constraints of 1939 America became a part of the circus family. Women certainly had more agency in the circus than they did in ordinary society. Many female circus stars like Lillian Leitzel, Bird Millman, and May Wirth wielded considerable power. And there were definitely women animal trainers like Mabel Stark, the renowned tiger trainer, and Barbara Woodcock, who trained elephants. Though I did embellish the strong woman act, the way Jabo describes Grace was influenced by the PBS special *The Circus*,[2] which I got to preview at the Circus Historical Society Convention.

All towns and cities are fictional except Chicago. The Chicago diner is fictional, as is Karaboo—though Karaboo was influenced by Baraboo, Wisconsin, where the Ringling Brothers Circus had its winter quarters until 1919.

The stories about Baby are also mostly true.[3] The Elephantoff act is almost entirely true, and Nico's save in that scene—announcing that Baby had a headache and was off to the pharmacy for aspirin—also comes from a true account, though it was an adult who invented this clever excuse, not a child.

1   lpaonline.org/faq-#Midget, accessed March 30, 2019.
2   "The Circus," *American Experience*, written, produced, and directed by Sharon Grimberg.
3   Vladimir L. Durov, *My Circus Animals* (Boston: Cambridge Riverdale Press, 1936), 52–73.

The tired tropes we think of when we say "circus" don't do justice to the performances of the late 1930s. In its heyday, the circus was an amazingly vibrant creative enterprise. The variety of routines was incredible, with each performer striving to create his or her own unique act. And many performers had multiple roles in the ring and behind the scenes. As one performer recalled, "Honey, no one does one thing in the circus."[4]

The circus glossary is accurate, though I've taken creative license with the definition of "John Robinson." Most sources say the term means to cut an act short because trouble is brewing. That said, specific circuses sometimes put their own spin on established words or coined their own expressions.

The Home for Friendless Children is fictional, but I did pull significant facts about the orphanage from the Davenport Main Library records of the Iowa Soldiers' Orphans' Home.

By the late 1930s and early 1940s, the Great Depression had taken its toll on Iowa, and the Soldiers' Orphans' Home census grew from the previous average of five hundred children to seven hundred. (Children were not always "true" orphans. Many had been brought to the home by families who no longer had the means to care for them.)

At the Soldiers' Orphans' Home, boys and girls were kept separate. Matrons sat at the doors of the dorms until

---

4 Connie Clausen, *I Love You Honey, but the Season's Over* (New York, Holt, Rinehart and Winston, 1961), 11.

the orphans fell asleep. Parents were sometimes told, "Do not contact your children. It only makes them sad." Relatives were allowed only one visit per month. They often sent stamps so the children could mail letters, but it isn't clear how often these stamps reached the orphans.[5]

I was especially interested in what happened when orphans misbehaved. Some were punished by being hit with straps, belts, or yardsticks. "Most kids [were] slapped around and paddled often."[6] This is horrifying but not surprising. In 1939, corporal punishment was fairly commonplace. If a child ran away from a place like the Home for Friendless Children, he or she might have been beaten. Or if it was the second offense, a child's head might have been shaved. Other punishments included being made to scrub floors and bathrooms or to sit in a chair for hours with feet flat on the floor. At the Soldiers' Orphans' Home, children who misbehaved were threatened with being sent to reform school.

"Every Monday the superintendent would come out at breakfast when everybody was eating, and he would have two lists, one was the boys that were going to Eldora and one was the girls that were going to Mitchellville. So if you were out of

---

5   June Schroeder, File OH 80, Soldiers' Orphans' Home Oral History Project, Davenport Public Library, Davenport, IA.
6   Gerald Van Cleve, Soldiers' Orphans' Home Oral History Project, Davenport Public Library, Davenport, IA.

line, your name appeared on that list. And I remember every time he came out with that list that I would shrink down in my chair just praying my name wasn't called."[7]

Though some resilient children thrived at the Soldiers' Orphans' Home, it was a grim existence for many. "The only thing that kept me going was I knew on Monday I would go to school."[8] And unfortunately, there were cruel matrons. One matron the children particularly disliked showed up in many of the oral histories I read. Another matron told the kids: "All you are is an expense to the taxpayers of Iowa."[9] But some matrons were kind. Erma Dalton, for example, wrote that she stopped working at the Soldiers' Orphans' Home because it was "so painful to see the children who said their parents were coming and to see them all dressed up & waiting & the parents never came!"[10]

I began this novel seven years ago with two characters: Lucy and Nico. I knew that Nico was a con man's apprentice and Lucy had selective mutism, but I couldn't figure out why Lucy refused to speak. I tried all kinds of backstories. None of them fit. The answer finally came when I happened on a

7   Annie Wittenmyer, Miscellaneous File, Soldiers' Orphans' Home Oral History Project, Davenport Public Library, Davenport, IA.

8   June Schroeder, File OH 80, Soldiers' Orphans' Home Oral History Project, Davenport Public Library, Davenport, IA.

9   June Schroeder, File OH 80, Soldiers' Orphans' Home Oral History Project, Davenport Public Library, Davenport, IA.

10 Erma Dalton, File OH 72, Soldiers' Orphans' Home Oral History Project, Davenport Public Library, Davenport, IA.

book called *Against Their Will: The Secret History of Medical Experimentation on Children in Cold War America.*

As with many little-known pieces of history, finding out the true story of the Fluency Study was challenging. Here's the truth so far as I can tell: The Fluency Study began with a man named Wendell Johnson, who struggled with stuttering his entire life. Wendell Johnson wanted to know why a child became a stutterer and how one might alleviate the problem. As he put it, "I became a speech pathologist because I needed one."[11] As a professor at the University of Iowa, he became a leader in the then relatively new field of speech pathology. It was his thesis that "Stuttering begins in the ear of the listener, not in the mouth of the child."[12] In other words, "The affliction is caused by the diagnosis."[13]

Johnson developed the Fluency Study to prove his thesis. The study subjects were orphans at the Iowa Soldiers' Orphans' Home. "The perfect test site was just an hour's drive from the campus: the Iowa Soldiers' Orphans' Home . . . they used that orphanage as a laboratory rat colony."[14]

11 Gretchen Reynolds, "The Stuttering Doctor's 'Monster Study,'" *The New York Times*, March 16, 2003, nytimes.com/2003/03/16/magazine/the-stuttering-doctor-s-monster-study .html.

12 Allen M. Hornblum, Judith L. Newman, and Gregory J. Dober, *Against Their Will: The Secret History of Medical Experimentation on Children in Cold War America* (New York, Palgrave Macmillan, 2013), 178.

13 Jim Dyer, "Ethics and Orphans: The Monster Study," *Mercury News*, June 10, 2001, front section.

14 Allen M. Hornblum, Judith L. Newman, and Gregory J. Dober, *Against Their Will: The Secret History of Medical Experimentation on Children in Cold War America* (New York, Palgrave Macmillan, 2013), 179.

Johnson designed the study; a graduate student named Mary Tudor helped him implement it. After going through files and examining "the speech of 256 orphans, she [Mary Tudor] and the other speech pathologists culled 22 subjects: 10 stutterers and 12 normal speakers. They paired the children based on similarities in age, sex, IQ, and fluency. Then they randomly assigned one from each pair to the control group and the other to the experimental group."[15]

The children in the experimental group were given constant negative reinforcement for their speech. "They were told that their speech was not normal at all, that they were beginning to stutter and that they must correct this immediately."[16] The children in the "control group" were given encouragement and positive reinforcement.

"Initially, children at the orphanage were delighted to receive this extra attention."[17] One of the student subjects, Mary Korlaske, remembered that "she had thought her sessions with Tudor were sponsored by the university to help her speak better."[18]

15 Allen M. Hornblum, Judith L. Newman, and Gregary J. Dober, *Against Their Will: The Secret History of Medical Experimentation on Children in Cold War America* (New York, Palgrave Macmillan, 2013), 179–180.

16 Gretchen Reynolds, "The Stuttering Doctor's 'Monster Study,'" *The New York Times*, March 16, 2003, nytimes.com/2003/03/16/magazine/the-stuttering-doctor-s-monster-study .html.

17 Allen M. Hornblum, Judith L. Newman, and Gregory J. Dober, *Against Their Will: The Secret History of Medical Experimentation on Children in Cold War America* (New York, Palgrave Macmillan, 2013), 180.

18 Jim Dyer, "Ethics and Orphans: The Monster Study," *Mercury News*, June 11, 2001, front section.

But soon that feeling changed dramatically. The children in the experimental group became deeply inhibited about their speech.

For "Case Number 11," a five-year-old who had no speaking issues initially but had been declared a "stutterer" by Johnson's team, the sessions were stressful from day one . . . additional "negative therapy" sessions with the girl worsened her speaking ability. The problem grew to the point where the little girl refused to speak . . . I [Mary Tudor] asked her if she was afraid of something . . . after some time she said, "Afraid I might stutter."[19]

According to the *New York Times*,[20] the experiment "failed completely" in actually creating stutterers. The *Mercury News* account, on the other hand, states that the orphans in the experimental group began to have an increase in speech interruptions.

Her (Mary Korlaske's) speech became jerky and hesitant, and she covered her face and slid down in

19 Allen M. Hornblum, Judith L. Newman, and Gregory J. Dober, *Against Their Will: The Secret History of Medical Experimentation on Children in Cold War America* (New York, Palgrave Macmillan, 2013), 181.
20 Gretchen Reynolds, "The Stuttering Doctor's 'Monster Study,'" *The New York Times*, March 16, 2003, nytimes.com/2003/03/16/magazine/the-stuttering-doctor-s-monster -study.html.

her chair. . . . She stuttered on words like "hand" and "got," and when she read "The Three Bears" she stuttered on "porridge," although months earlier she had little trouble reading the story. . . . Over the course of four months, they [Mary Korlaske's speech interruptions] had more than doubled. The other children who were in the same experimental group as Mary Korlaske showed similar effects. . . . Nine-year-old Elizabeth Ostert and twelve-year-old Phillip Spieker saw their grades plummet because they became afraid to talk in class . . . [Hazel Potter] developed mannerisms characteristic of some stutterers, such as snapping her fingers to get a word out.[21]

I have surmised that a child like Mary Korlaske would have become extremely important to Wendell Johnson and Mary Tudor, as she proved his theory. In any case, Johnson continued to believe in his thesis, and so, apparently, did many others. According to the *New York Times* article, "Johnson's theory dominated until the 1970s, when speech pathologists began to reexamine its premise."[22] And though researchers who analyze

---

21 Jim Dyer, "Ethics and Orphans: The Monster Study," *Mercury News*, June 11, 2001, front section.
22 Jim Dyer, "Ethics and Orphans: The Monster Study," *Mercury News*, June 11, 2001, front section.

the study now strongly disagree with his conclusion, he thought the experiment proved he was right.

Since I am writing fiction, I elected to have Lucy develop mutism from being in the experimental group. All the accounts I read stated that partial mutism occurred in some of the children in the experimental group as a result of being exposed to the constant barrage of criticism. I have her hesitate and stutter slightly once she musters the courage to begin speaking again. And I didn't have her hesitate or stutter at all when reading aloud or singing. It is my understanding that some kids stutter when reading out loud. Others do not. And many stutterers do not stutter when they sing. In any case, it didn't seem like there was a cookie-cutter response to being in the experimental group. So I imagined the way my character might have handled this situation.

By the time the experiment was complete, the parallels between the Fluency Study and experiments on human subjects in Nazi Germany were all too obvious, and the study results were buried.

> During the war years, some of [Johnson's] graduate students, concerned about the ethics of the orphan study, had begun calling it the "Monster Experiment" or the "Monster Study." They warned him that although the experiment was hardly unique in having used orphans as subjects, it was a particularly sensitive time: In the aftermath of World War II,

observers might draw comparisons to Nazi experiments on human subjects, which could destroy his career.[23]

The results of the Fluency Study were never published.

Though Matron Mackinac and Matron Grundy are entirely fictional, it is true that Mary Tudor asked the teachers and matrons at the Soldiers' Orphans' Home to continue criticism of children in the experimental group between her sessions. For the kids in this group, the torment was unrelenting.

I don't know why the Soldiers' Orphans' Home offered up orphans for experimentation. The increase in the census had spread resources quite thin, and I surmised that monetary gifts from the university might have made them willing to allow the university to experiment on the children, but this is pure speculation on my part.

It is not speculation that the University of Iowa regretted using the children from the Soldiers' Orphan Home for the fluency study.

On June 14, 2001, "University of Iowa officials issued a formal apology . . . for an experiment conducted by their speech pathology department in 1939, in which orphans were induced to stutter."[24]

---

23 Jim Dyer, "Ethics and Orphans: The Monster Study," *Mercury News,* June 11, 2001, front section.
24 Jim Dyer, "Ethics and Orphans: The Monster Study," *Mercury News,* June 14, 2001, front section.

In 2001, six orphans who were unwilling participants in the Fluency Study sued the state of Iowa for the damage incurred. In 2007 the case was settled. The orphans won.

"The state (Iowa) has agreed to pay $925,000 to the unwitting subjects of an infamous 1930s stuttering experiment—orphans who were badgered and belittled as children by University of Iowa researchers trying to induce speech impediments."[25]

Money doesn't begin to compensate these children for what they went through. Still, how often do orphans prevail in a battle against a big university?

25 nbcnews.com/id/20327467/ns/health-health_care/t/iowa-pay-subjects-k-stuttering-study/#.XAGKBy2ZP-Y, accessed November 30, 2018.

GLOSSARY OF CIRCUS TERMS

advance man: A person who plasters circus billboards in advance of the circus's arrival.

backyard: The area of the circus where the performers and working men live and props and costumes are kept. Backstage in the circus.

baggage stock: Horses used for hauling.

big top: The main performing tent.

boiling up: Washing clothes and taking baths.

boss canvas man: The man in charge of setting up the circus tents and taking them down.

bull: An elephant.

bull girl: A girl who works with elephants.

bull hand: A person who works with elephants.

candy butcher: A person who works at a concession stand.

cook tent: The tent where meals are made and eaten.

first-of-May: A worker new to the circus. (Named after the time of the year when new circus workers generally arrive.)

fixer: A member of the circus whose job it is to make financial amends for any damage caused by a circus performer.

grind: The spiel or polished talk of a person who stands outside the circus trying to get new customers to buy tickets.

John Robinson: The code word for "danger" in the circus. (Not a universal term.)

jump: The move from one stand or circus location to another.

liberty horse: A riderless horse trained to perform by verbal commands.

outside talker: A person who stands outside the circus trying to get new customers to pay the admission fee and go inside.

pie car: The cooking or dining car on a circus train.

red-lighting: The practice of throwing a circus worker or performer off the train for bad behavior.

ring stock: Performing horses.

roustabout: A circus workman or laborer.

route card: The card that shows the schedule of cities or towns (known as stands) where a circus will perform.

sawdust in your shoes: A person who has sawdust in their shoes loves the circus so much she or he wants to join it.

spec: The giant opening pageant of a circus.

stand: A city or town where the circus performs.

target girl: A lady the knife thrower uses as a target for his knives. Knives are generally thrown around the target girl's body.

tenting work: Putting up or taking down circus tents.

winter quarters: The place where the circus stays off season to regroup and retrain.

Acknowledgments

· ·

Orphan Eleven would not be the book you hold in your hands if not for the many skilled readers who offered their time and thoughtful comments on draft after draft after draft.

A huge thank you to McKenzie Beery, Sarah Gerton, Elizabeth Harding, Lisa Leach, Sarah Little, Alyssa Maria Mignone, Lee Uniacke, Kristin Schulz, Shaughnessy Miller, and Erica Stone.

I would like to thank the Circus Historical Society and the many fine circus historians who encouraged and inspired me. Thank you to the Robert L. Parkinson Library and Research Center in Baraboo, Wisconsin, for allowing me access to your incredible archives, and to Katie Reinhardt at the Richardson-Sloane Special Collections Center of the Davenport Public Library for helping me find information about the Soldiers' Orphans' Home.

My critique group was instrumental in helping me with this book. Their encouragement and early love of Dilly (*"When is Dilly coming back? We need more Dilly"*) made me realize the power of this character. Thank you, Elizabeth Partridge, Diane Frasier, Marissa Moss, Pamela S. Turner, Eleanor Vincent, and most especially Emily Polsby.

Thank you to Iacopo Bruno for creating a cover I

absolutely adore and to Leslie Mechanic, who knew he was the right artist for this book.

Thank you to my conscientious copyediting team, Alison Kolani, Colleen Fellingham, and Annette Szlachta-McGinn. And thank you to my publicist, Emily Bamford, who does a great job getting the word out about my books.

A gigantic thanks to my editors, Wendy Lamb and Dana Carey. Wendy's comments on an early draft changed the course of this book in dramatic and affecting ways. Her perceptions about the deeper themes helped me to understand and shape what I'd written. And Dana's attention to pacing and her kid-friendly focus made every chapter more fun. Thank you, Wendy Lamb Books, for taking such tender care of *Orphan Eleven*.

About the Author

GENNIFER CHOLDENKO is the author of the Newbery Honor–winning *New York Times* bestseller *Al Capone Does My Shirts* and the wildly popular *Al Capone Shines My Shoes, Al Capone Does My Homework,* and *Al Capone Throws Me a Curve.* She also wrote *One-Third Nerd, Chasing Secrets,* and a bunch of other wacky books about dinosaurs and stuff. She grew up in Los Angeles, but she lives in the San Francisco Bay Area, where she spends most of her time thinking about elephants.

genifercholdenko.com